SEPTEMBER

(The Christina Dandridge Story—A companion novel to the *Been So Long* series)

I0672916

Adrienne Thompson

Pink Cashmere Publishing
Arkansas, USA

Cover art by AA Thompson (**thompson9699@gmail.com**)

Printed in the United States of America

First Printing 2015

ISBN: 0692463100

ISBN-13: 978-0-692-46310-9

All praises to the Most High God, without whom I could not write a single word.
Thank You, Lord, for giving me stories to write and readers to read them.

To my readers, I cannot thank you enough for spending your hard-earned money on the stuff that comes from my mind. I pray all of you will be blessed with more than you can stand!

A special thank you to Tonja Tate, Nicole Sharon, and Barbara Joe Williams.

Trigger Warning:
This book contains depictions of child abuse and neglect, and sexual assault.

RIP to all of our brothers and sisters who've lost their lives due to senseless violence.
#blacklivesmatter
#sayhername

"The Lord is near to those that have a broken heart, and he saves those who have a contrite spirit."
Psalms 34:18

SOUNDTRACK:

"C'mon Children" *Earth Wind & Fire*
"Sweet Sassy Lady" *Earth Wind & Fire*
"That's the Way of the World" *Earth Wind & Fire*
"Runnin'" *Earth Wind & Fire*
"Evil" *Earth Wind & Fire*
"Mom" *Earth Wind & Fire*
"Inner City Blues (Make Me Wanna Holler)" *Marvin Gaye*
"Departure" *Earth Wind & Fire*
"Sad Tomorrows" *Marvin Gaye*
"Remember the Children" *Earth Wind & Fire*
"Reasons" *Earth Wind & Fire*
"You Went Away" *Earth Wind & Fire*
"Fantasy" *Earth Wind & Fire*
"Sunshine" *Earth Wind & Fire*
"Black Man" *Stevie Wonder*
"Getaway" *Earth Wind & Fire*
"The Changing Times" *Earth Wind & Fire*
"Where Have All the Flowers Gone" *Earth Wind & Fire*
"Deep In It" *Marvin Gaye*
"Save the Children" *Marvin Gaye*
"Devotion" *Earth Wind & Fire*
"Power" *Earth Wind & Fire*
"Shining Star" *Earth Wind & Fire*
"All About Love" *Earth Wind & Fire*
"Keep Your Head to the Sky" *Earth Wind & Fire*
"After the Love Has Gone" *Earth Wind & Fire*
"Spread Your Love" *Earth Wind & Fire*
"You" *Earth Wind & Fire*
"The Speed of Love" *Earth Wind & Fire*
"Here Today and Gone Tomorrow" *Earth Wind & Fire*
"Build Your Nest" *Earth Wind & Fire*
"System of Survival" *Earth Wind & Fire*
"They Don't See" *Earth Wind & Fire*

Check out the September Book Soundtrack on YouTube

We sat there together and stared at those boxes like they were a TV show or a movie. Finally, Cleo opened one of them and peered inside.

"Just books," she said.

She slid the box to the side and opened the other three boxes. She released a frustrated sigh. "All books!"

I frowned as I grabbed one of the boxes and pulled it to me. I began to empty its contents—*Treasure Island, Moby Dick, Little Women*. Our mother was nothing if not well read.

"I'm sorry, Cleo. I didn't mean to disappoint you. I just thought…"

Cleo shook her low-hung head. "It's okay. I knew better than to get my hopes up."

I knew how she felt. I absently opened my mother's copy of *Moby Dick* and as I thumbed through it, my eyes widened. "It's a journal," I whispered.

"You say something?" Cleo asked.

I dropped *Moby Dick* and picked up *Treasure Island*, then *Lord of the Flies*. I shoved *Little Women* into Cleo's face. "They're not books! They're her journals!! She glued these book covers onto them to disguise them! Look!"

Cleo flipped through the book, her eyes wide with wonder. Then we grabbed each other and hugged and giggled like we'd just discovered a buried treasure, like we'd uncovered some delightful secret.

We spent the next hour organizing the books by the dates written inside. Then, after eating lunch with our family, we begged them not to disturb us and we sat down and began to read our mother's words aloud to each other.

"I was born September 5, 1960 in England, Arkansas. My mother is white. My father is black, and me? I'm nothing."

That's how the very first entry in the first journal began. And the remainder of her words read similarly—like she was chronicling her life for someone. Was that what she'd done? Did she know that one day Cleo and I would be reading her words, her life's story?

—from *Been So Long III (Whatever It Takes)*

Prologue

I am dying. That is a blunt way of putting it, but it's the truth. I'm dying from lung cancer. I've basically smoked myself to death. I'm responsible for my own demise, to be honest. So, I'm not angry; there would be no sense in it if I were. No, I'm not angry, but I'm very aware that my time is running out, and at the same time, I feel like there is too much time on my hands. Too much time for me to think, to remember, and to regret. My life keeps playing over and over again in my mind like an old raggedy video tape that skips some parts and repeats others.

In an attempt to delete the images and silence the voices in my head, I began to write my story and hid it between the jackets and spines of some of my favorite books. If you've found this particular part of my story, you've found my deepest secrets, the ones I didn't intend for anyone to ever know about. I omitted some things from the other journals—parts that included my brother—because it was too painful for me to write about him at first, but this journal tells my story in its entirety—my story and his story. I left this journal with my dear friend, Dulcina, for her to keep apart from the others. For her to keep from my daughters, from everyone. But if you've found it, then you must be meant to read it. Read it carefully. Learn from it. Tell others about my life.

1

"C'mon Children"

My name is Christina Dandridge, but my family always called me Chrissy.

My parents met on my grandparents' farm in England, Arkansas. At the time, my mother, Patty Dandridge, was 21 and had just finished college. She had returned home to her family and a promised teaching job. My father was a farmhand. His name was Kenny Ray Greene and he was tall and dark cedar-colored and the same age as her. And he was so handsome. He had the nicest dark brown eyes, a wide nose, and square jaw. His thick hair was always neatly cut and he was smart, too. My mother said that from the moment she saw him, she fell in love with him.

My mother was petite with dull brown hair, green eyes, and pallid skin that refused to tan and only burned in the summer sun. I can't say that she was all that pretty and I never heard anyone else say it, either, not even her own family members. But I guess she was pretty to my father, because as the story is told, he fell for her pretty quickly, too, despite her mousiness. Or maybe it wasn't her beauty that he saw. Maybe it was just that she was forbidden fruit—a young white woman in the south.

It was Arkansas and it was the 1960s, so to say their love was forbidden would be an understatement. They had to sneak around to be together and from what my mother told me, I was conceived one cold December evening in my grandparents' barn. When my grandparents found out, they were heartbroken, but they still loved their only daughter and allowed her and my father to live in a little house they owned back in the woods, though they refused to visit her or allow my father into their home. Two years later, my brother, Kenny Ray, was born. We were beautiful children, both possessing tawny skin, clear green eyes, and thick sandy hair that fell in ringlets to our shoulders. Our parents never married, and life was a struggle for them. The local school fired my mother after word got out about her black lover and mixed kids. So we lived on the wages my father earned from working on my grandparents' farm, which wasn't much to say the least.

When I was five and Kenny was three, our father left us to go up north to look for work. We stayed in that little house back in the woods and waited for him. As the days turned into weeks which turned into months with no word from him, I saw my mother change. She was known to have mood swings from time to time, but that got even worse and her occasional smile faded as her patience with her condition and with me and Kenny began to run thin. After a year passed without a single word from my father, she decided to go up north to find him.

That was the first time she left us behind with relatives. The year was 1966.

We went to live with our father's mother, Grandma Orene Greene.

2

Grandma Orene was tall and big and dark and downright scary to look at. She looked like she enjoyed whooping kids and those big hands didn't look like they'd show us any mercy if we got out of line. I was so scared when Mama pulled us out of the car and stood us in the yard in front of her, I almost peed on myself.

But then she opened her wide mouth and gave us a smile so warm that I couldn't help but smile right back at her. Then she started laughing—a big, belly laugh. And I laughed, too.

"Lord, I ain't seent these two babies in so long, I almost forgot how they looked! Beautiful chirrin', they are. Just look at 'em. Just like two little peaches with that orange skin. And those green eyes! Y'all come on over here and give your granny a hug."

I was the first to move. I walked over to her and let her wrap her big, heavy, warm arms around me. I will never forget how she smelled—like talcum powder and fried chicken. From the moment I met Grandma Orene and felt what it was like to be in her arms, I fell in love with her.

My brother was always shy and I think our grandmother's imposing appearance frightened him, too. After she let me go and waited for Kenny to walk over to her, he just stood there with his head hung low. I could tell he was about to cry. My first thought was to call him a cry-baby, and then I realized he was just four and all he knew was our Mama. He wanted to be with her and so did I. But if she had to leave, I had a feeling we were going to be in good hands with Grandma Orene.

I walked over to him and wrapped my arm around his shoulder. "Come on, Kenny Ray," I whispered. "It's all right."

Kenny Ray shook me off of him and ran to our mother. He gripped her skinny legs and cried and shouted, "Mommy, don't go!"

Mama looked down at him with tears in her eyes. She rubbed her hand over his hair and then squatted down to face him. She pulled him into her arms and whispered, "Be a big boy, Kenny Ray. I'm just going to bring Daddy home. I'll be back before you know it."

Kenny Ray clung tightly to her, cried louder. He didn't believe her. Neither did I. Why would we believe her when the last person who was supposed to come right back was our daddy?

Mama had to pry Kenny's arms from around her neck and when she stood to her feet, I could see the wet spot on her blouse left behind by Kenny's tears. Kenny's cries became shrill and louder as Mama backed away from us, moving toward the car door. Grandma Orene stepped forward, and when she wrapped her thick fingers around Kenny's little arm, his knees buckled and landed on the gravel of the makeshift driveway that made up most of our grandmother's front yard. His cries transformed from shrill sobs to pained wails.

I reached for him but Grandma Orene shook her head. "You let me take care of him, sugar," she said warmly. "Now come on here, big boy. I got some cake in here and I think you'll like it. It's chocolate. Your mama told me you love chocolate cake."

Kenny's wailing stopped almost the second she spoke the words "chocolate cake". His wet eyes widened and he stood to his feet.

Our grandmother turned to me and winked. "Let's go get us some cake, Chrissy."

I smiled as I followed her into the old, paint-stripped house.

***

Grandma Orene's house was larger than the little house in the woods where Kenny and I had spent our lives up until that point, but it was full of furniture and knick-knacks. It smelled like food and was so warm, much warmer than our house. It was an old house, but the floors didn't creak like at our house and the air didn't seep in under the doors and the windows didn't rattle when the wind blew. The furniture was old, but not raggedy. The couch sagged but was covered with a clean quilt. The coffee table was chipped, but there wasn't a speck of dirt on it. The house was lived-in, but not run down. It had taken on the characteristics of a true home rather than just a building.

When I walked into the kitchen and saw all of that food on the table, I couldn't believe it. I had never seen so much food in one place and intended for one meal in my whole life! Fried chicken, greens, pinto beans, cornbread, boiled okra, potato salad, and of course, a triple-stacked chocolate cake with chocolate icing. I looked over at Kenny whose eyes had grown so wide, I thought they were going to pop out of his head.

"We gon' eat all this?" he asked excitedly.

"As much of it as you want," Grandma Orene answered. "Now, go wash your hands over at the sink. We gon' eat soon as your Aunt Joyce and your Uncle Larry get back."

I took Kenny's hand and inched toward the sink. "Who is they?" I asked.

"They your daddy's sister and brother. Now go on and wash them hands."

"Where they at?" I said as I turned the water on in the faucet and lathered my hands with soap.

"Down the road a bit. They be back shortly."

I nodded. "You my daddy's mama, right?"

She smiled at me and nodded. "Yes, I am, smart girl."

"Where his daddy at?"

A sadness swiftly filled her eyes. "He long been dead, baby. Long been dead. The white man took him from me and my chirrin' a long time ago, said he was too uppity, too proud. Lynched him back in the woods," she said and then turned back to the stove. "I sho' do miss him. He was a good man, good and handsome." She shook her head.

I felt a little sad, too, as I helped Kenny wash his hands. We were drying them off when we heard the front door open. Kenny and I stood by the sink and watched as our daddy walked into the kitchen. My eyes grew large and Kenny's mouth dropped open as he said, "Daddy!" He took off running, but Daddy stopped him and held up his hands.

"Wait a minute, now. I ain't nobody's daddy," he said. As soon as he spoke, I knew he wasn't our daddy. His voice was different, but they must've been twins.

"You ain't got no kids that you know of," our grandmother said as she rolled her eyes at the man. "Kids, this your Uncle Larry, your daddy's brother."

"They twins?" I asked.

Grandma Orene stepped closer to me and Kenny and pushed us toward the table. "Y'all go on and sit down. We gon' eat in a minute."

I nodded. "Y'all twins?" I asked again, this time directing my question to my uncle.

He shook his head as he reached into the pocket of his denim jacket and pulled out a red and white pack of cigarettes. He placed a cigarette in his mouth and said, "Naw. I'm a year older than Kenny."

Grandma Orene walked over to him and smacked the cigarette out of his mouth. I watched as it hit the floor. "Is you done lost your mind? You know you can't smoke up in here. I ain't finna have that smell all up in my curtains."

"Ain't no worse than them chitlins' you love to cook all the time," he muttered as he bent over and picked up the cigarette. He brushed it off with his finger and placed it back in his mouth. "Ain't nothing wrong with cigarettes, Mama."

"Larry John, I don't give a damn if cigarettes'll make you grow ten feet tall. You ain't gon' smoke 'em up in here! Now, if you so dead set on doing what you wanna do, then take yourself on down that road to your wife. Otherwise, take your black behind out back and smoke."

"She ain't my wife."

"May as well be. Y'all shacking, ain't you?"

"Not no more. That's why I'm here."

"He here 'cause that girl put him out, and I don't blame her. He can't keep a job to save his life. All he do is drink and sleep," said a woman as she stepped into the kitchen. She was beautiful with big, round eyes and long, straight, jet-black hair. She was wearing a short red dress and a short fur jacket. She had on red high heel shoes with lipstick to match. She smirked and then her eyes settled on me and Kenny. "These Kenny's kids?" she asked.

"Sho' is," Grandma Orene said. "Ain't they some pretty little things?"

The woman shrugged. "Yeah. Can't believe they came from that homely white girl. All these colored girls around here just crazy about him and he chooses to be with that Plain Jane."

"Joyce, mind your manners. That's they mama you talking about," Grandma said in a huff.

I couldn't have cared less about her talking about my mother. I was too captivated by her—*my aunt*. She was the most beautiful woman I had ever seen in my life.

"Well, one thing's for sure," my aunt said, "it's a good thing he left her. I'm surprised he ain't get himself lynched for shacking up with her."

"Humph," Uncle Larry said. "He woulda if her family had cared about her. I heard she had to work her way through college. Her folks too poor to care who she lay with."

Aunt Joyce rolled her eyes. "As if you can talk. It's a wonder some Negro ain't strung you up, many folks' wives you done had. You and Kenny Ray gon' be the death of Mama."

"You gon' let her talk crazy about me like that, Mama?" our uncle asked.

"Ain't nothing crazy about the truth, Larry," our aunt said as she took a seat at the table next to me. She smelled like flowers. "What you cook, Mama? I'm hungry as a stray dog."

"Just like them dogs you hang around with, huh? You ain't made life easy for me, either, Joyce," Grandma said.

Our aunt didn't answer; she just glanced at her mother and then dropped her eyes.

"Larry, sit down so we can eat. Then I need for you to help me set them up somewhere to sleep, Joyce," Grandma Orene ordered.

"Yes, ma'am," our uncle and aunt said in unison.

2

"Sweet Sassy Lady"

That first night, Aunt Joyce spread a bunch of quilts on top of each other on the floor of our grandmother's bedroom and that's where me and my brother slept. Once we settled down on our pallet, Grandma Orene covered us with two more quilts. I'd never slept in such a warm, comfortable way before. We were so full from dinner that it didn't take long for us to fall asleep. I remember wishing that me and Kenny Ray could stay there forever.

The next morning was a Sunday. Grandma got up early and fixed breakfast and after searching through the rags me and Kenny Ray had for clothes, she decided to let us stay home with Aunt Joyce. Uncle Larry had left before breakfast.

"You need to be up in the church, yourself," our grandmother said to our aunt, "but I can't take these chirrin' to da Lord's house looking throwed away, so you gon' hafta stay here wit' 'em. I'ma have to get them some church clothes. Now be sure to stay here wit' 'em, Joyce.

They can't be left alone."

Aunt Joyce rolled her eyes. "I look like I'm crazy or something? I know they can't be left alone."

"You don't *look* crazy, but as soon as Arthur Lee Jenkins darken the door, you lose your mind."

"Me and Arthur got something special. You wouldn't understand."

"Humph, from what I heard, he got something special wit' a whole buncha women."

"Just gossip. Empty words from the mouths of miserable, man-less women. I'm surprised you listen to that, being the church woman you are and everything."

Grandma looked a little embarrassed. "You and that smart mouth. Explain to me why you let that man hit you since you so smart."

Aunt Joyce shifted her eyes to the floor and didn't reply.

"Just watch these babies while I'm gone," Grandma said.

"I will." She turned her attention to us and said, "Y'all two come on. I need some air."

Minutes after our grandmother left for church on foot, Kenny Ray and I were playing with an old red wagon in her front yard while our aunt sat on the front steps, reading a book. I stared at her as I pulled Kenny Ray in the wagon. He was giggling up a storm, having the time of his life from his seat in that old wagon as I pulled him over dirt and gravel and exposed tree roots. Fun wasn't something we experienced too often at home with our parents. We were too poor for toys, and they were too miserable together to even attempt to entertain us. And after our father disappeared, things only got worse. There were days at a time when our mother would sit in a corner of our little house, curled up like a baby and crying like one, too. And if she wasn't crying, she was yelling, screaming at me and Kenny Ray about how we made her life a living hell—blaming us for her misery. I didn't understand what we'd done, and it always scared Kenny Ray when she got like that. Even at my young age, I was forced to comfort him.

I watched as Aunt Joyce sat there with her eyes glued to the book. When Kenny Ray finally grew tired of riding in the wagon and decided to gather some rocks, I walked over to the porch and sat down beside my aunt. I peered at the words on the page, which at the time, looked like a jumble of letters to me. I hadn't started school yet, and I couldn't read at all.

"What's that?" I asked.

She looked up at me and sighed as if she'd hoped I'd disappeared or something. "A book. Ain't you ever seen one before?"

I shook my head. "No."

"Yo' mama went to college. She ain't got no books?"

I shook my head again. "No," I repeated.

"Wasn't she a teacher or something?"

I shrugged.

"She or your daddy ever read to you?"

"No."

She frowned. "What a miserable life. No books? I'd die without my books."

I peered at the words again. "What it say?"

She smiled slightly. "Want me to read you some?"

I nodded.

She flipped to the first page of the book and began to read what I would later know were the opening lines of *A Tale of Two Cities*. I had no idea what any of it meant, but I liked the way it sounded, and I liked the way her voice wrapped around the words, giving them life.

When she reached a stopping point, she closed the book and smiled at me. "Did you like it?"

I nodded. "Where you get it from?"

She placed the book in her lap. "Well, most folks go to the colored library to check out books, but I got a good friend who buys mine for me."

I was just about to ask her if she would read some more when a car rushed into the yard, narrowly missing my brother who'd taken his rock search to the edge of the property. I rushed to get him and bring him closer to the house as a white man stepped out of the car and slammed the door shut.

As I pulled Kenny Ray toward the porch, Aunt Joyce stood to her feet and with her hands on her wide hips, said, "May I help you?" rather defiantly.

"You don't know who I am?" the man asked as he approached her.

"What? You think 'cause you white I'm supposed to know who you are? I'm sorry, *Mr. White Man*, but the whole damn world don't revolve around y'all like y'all think it do. So no, I don't know who you are, and you ain't got no right to be on my mama's property. You almost ran over my nephew!"

He turned and seemed to notice me and Kenny Ray for the first time. "He's my nephew, too. I'm Teddy Dandridge, Patty's brother."

I had never seen him before, or at least I didn't *remember* seeing him. He was tall and skinny with the same green eyes and dull brown hair as my mother, but his skin was more sallow than hers. He definitely wasn't much to look at, either. As a matter of fact, with his hooked nose, he was even less attractive than my mother. And there was something about his eyes that bothered me. As cordial as he was being with Aunt Joyce, something about him made my skin crawl. I pulled my little brother closer to me, never taking my eyes off of my newly-discovered uncle.

"Humph, well again I say, how can I help you?" Aunt Joyce asked. Uncle Teddy's explanation had done nothing to quench her irritation.

"Uh, Patty called and asked me to come check on the kids since y'all ain't got no phone for her to check herself."

"She leaves her kids behind, and she got the nerve to be worried about them?"

"Their daddy left them, too," he said with a little irritation in his voice.

"Hell, everyone know my brother is sorry. A sorry daddy is one thing, but a sorry mother? That's just a damn shame."

He shrugged. "I can see they're fine. I'll let her know."

"Mm-hmm, and let her know that it'd be nice if someone helped my mama with the grocery bill. These kids eat like they ain't never seen food before. Been here one day and they about to eat my mama out of house and home."

Uncle Teddy dug in his pocket and pulled out some money then handed it to her. She tucked it in her bra and didn't bother to thank him. He stood there for a few minutes and then climbed back into his car and left.

"Come on, kids. Let's go back inside. It's cold as hell out here," Aunt Joyce said.

We followed her back into the house where she warmed up the previous day's dinner for us to eat for lunch. I made sure not to eat too much. I liked being there and I wanted her to read to me some more, so I didn't want to get into any trouble with her. I tried to get Kenny Ray to slow down his eating, too, but it was no use. When our grandmother finally made it back home, it was getting close to dark, and I remember wondering what in the world church was and why it took all day to do it.

3

"That's the Way of the World"

We had been living with our grandmother for almost three months and hadn't heard from our mother since her brother showed up unannounced that day. Kenny Ray often cried for her, but I didn't really miss her at all. Who would miss being screamed and yelled at? Who would miss being cold and hungry? Not me.

I loved living with Grandma Orene and eating her good cooking. I loved the way she cooked smothered cabbage with onions and smoked sausage or the way she made her hamburger meat stew, which she called soup, with tons of stewed tomatoes in it. I loved when Uncle Larry would go fishing and bring back a bunch of fish—catfish and brim—and how Grandma Orene would let me help her roll the cut up pieces of fish in cornmeal. I loved how the grease in her big cast iron skillet would pop and how the whole house would smell like fried fish. Me and Kenny Ray would giggle at how much hot sauce Uncle Larry would pour on his fish. If he was in a good mood, he'd smile at us and say, "I like a little fish with my hot sauce." It took me years to understand that joke.

Then there were my grandmother's buttery tea cakes, her heavy chess pie, her addictive banana pudding, and her moist pound cake. We ate good every day, which was a far cry from the bologna and crackers we almost always had for dinner at our parents' house.

I loved listening to my grandmother hum as she cooked or cleaned. I loved sitting in her lap while she told me stories about my daddy as a little boy. And when she was finally able to get me and Kenny Ray some decent clothes, I loved going to church with her. I loved to hear the choir sing and the older ladies moan while the preacher yelled and whooped.

But more than anything, I loved being around my Aunt Joyce. She was so pretty and smart and tough. I loved it when she talked crazy to Uncle Larry, because I really didn't like him most of the time since he was almost always in a bad mood. All he seemed to do was smoke cigarettes and sneak a swig from a whiskey bottle that always looked full to me. He was so lazy that Aunt Joyce and Grandma Orene had to gather wood for the stove. But he was always front and center at the dinner table when it was time to eat.

But Aunt Joyce, she was wonderful. She would read to me every day. She even taught me a few words and she started teaching me to write my ABC's. She would tell me about grown up stuff, too, like how much she loved that Arthur man and how no one understood them and how they were going to get married one day. She also said she really wanted to go to college but that Grandma Orene didn't have the money for it. She hoped that maybe she could start college after she married Arthur since he was rich. I didn't like Arthur from the first time I saw him. As a matter of fact, I felt the same way about him as I felt about my Uncle Teddy…

One weekend, Grandma Orene went on a trip with her church and left me and Kenny Ray behind with our aunt and uncle. Uncle Larry spent the weekend either drunk and asleep or just drunk. Aunt Joyce spent most of her time sitting on the porch or staring out the window. She was so nervous about something that when I asked her to read to me, she yelled at me. Tears welled up in my eyes, and I took her book of Negro poetry, sat on the porch, and turned the pages, trying to read it for myself, but it's kind of hard to read when you can only recognize ten or so words. When a shiny red car pulled into the yard, I closed the book and stared at it. It was the prettiest car I had ever seen in my entire short life!

The man who stepped out of the car was just as pretty and shiny in his black suit and fedora. He was very light-skinned. As a matter of fact, he could've passed for white had the hair peeking from underneath his hat not been so kinky. He smiled, elongating his thin moustache, as he approached the house.

He pulled his hat from his head and nodded at me. "Well, hey there, little peach. Is Miss Joyce in?"

I just stared at him.

"Hmm, you don't talk, huh?"

"Arthur Lee!" Aunt Joyce squealed as the screen door flew open and she rushed down the steps and into his arms.

He laughed. "Girl, you gonna knock me over."

She kissed him all over his face. "It's been forever! How was Chicago this time? What you bring me?"

He chuckled and shook his head as he fixed his eyes on me. "See here, little peach. This all grown women think about—*gifts*."

"I asked you about your trip first," she said.

"It was good, baby. Made some good money, drank some good whiskey, made some new friends."

"Okay… what you bring me?" she persisted.

He grinned as he backed away from her and reached through the driver side window of his car. He pulled out a big brown package and handed it to her. She squealed again, kissed him on the mouth, and ripped the package open right there in the yard, tossing brown paper and twine around like it was leaves and dirt. Inside were four books. She smiled as she read the titles aloud: "*Little Women, The Bell Jar, To Kill a Mockingbird,* and *The Autobiography of Malcolm X.* Oh, thank you, Arthur!" She hugged him again.

"Not so fast. Look what else I got." He reached back into the car and pulled out the prettiest bottle I'd ever seen.

"Perfume?!" Aunt Joyce said. She snatched the bottle from him, pulled out the plunger, and held it to her nose. "Oh, it smells so good. I can't wait to wear it for you."

He leaned in close to her and kissed her on the neck. "No time like the present. You can wear it for me now." He gripped her around the waist and stared into her eyes.

She giggled. "But my mama is gone, and my brother is passed out on the sofa, drunk. I gotta watch these kids."

"I don't see but one kid."

"Oh, yeah. The other one is taking a nap."

"Hell, this one look like she old enough to watch herself. She grown in the eyes. Come with me for a little while, baby. You know I missed you."

"I missed you, too, baby. But I can't leave them here like that."

"Can't we go to your room, then? I really need some time with you." He kissed her. "Come on. We can leave the door open if you want."

She sighed. "Hold on." She turned to me and said, "Come on, Chrissy. Let me make you a snack, and I want you to sit at that table until I tell you that you can get up, okay?"

I nodded. "Okay."

She fixed me a sandwich and a cup of milk, and then she and Arthur went into her room and pulled the door to, leaving it open just a crack. I sat at the table and ate the sandwich and drank the milk, and then I had to pee, but the bathroom was next to Aunt Joyce's room and I didn't want her to get mad at me for disobeying her. So I sat there listening to muffled sounds of bumping and moaning—the same sounds my parents used to make—as they floated through the house. I sat there and listened and held my pee for as long as I could before finally easing out of the chair and quietly walking to the bathroom. I peed but didn't flush the toilet. As I passed back by her door, I decided to stop and peek through the crack at them. It looked like they were fighting or something. I wondered if he was hogging the covers. Back when me and Kenny Ray had to sleep together in the little bed in our parents' house, he used to hog the covers all the time and I used to hate that. He slept wild, too—always kicking me in my side. It looked like Arthur Lee was a very wild sleeper, and he must've been hurting Aunt Joyce because she was moaning real loud.

By the time they finished, I was back in my seat at the table. I heard Arthur Lee's car pull out of the yard, but I still didn't move. I waited for Aunt Joyce to come and get me, but after waiting for what felt like a really long time, I finally decided to get up and go looking for her. She was still in her room, sitting on the side of the bed wearing a robe. And she was crying.

"Aunt Joyce, can I get up from the table, now?" I asked softly from the doorway.

She looked up at me. "Look like you done already got up."

"I'm sorry. I waited like you said."

She nodded.

"Why you crying?"

She stared at me for a moment. "How old are you, Chrissy?"

"Six."

"You young, but I guess you ain't never too young to learn. Come sit down beside me."

I walked into the room and thought to myself that it really smelled weird, like my parents' room would smell after they got through fighting in their bed. I really didn't like that smell, and I guess my little face showed it.

"Why you got your nose turned up?" she asked.

"'Cause it smell in here."

She laughed and then pulled me into a hug. She'd never hugged me before. "I'ma tell you something, and I want you to listen and never forget, you hear me?"

I nodded.

"Men ain't nothing, Chrissy. I don't care what man it is or where he came from, he ain't gon' be nothing. They all no good. They only think about themselves, and to survive in this world, you gotta only think about yourself. If you gon' be with a man, be sure he got something to give you. Don't give him nothing unless he gon' give you something first."

"Like books?"

She smiled. "Books, money, whatever. You gotta use them, because they sho' gon' use you. And don't fall in love. Love turns you into a fool. You a smart girl—smart and pretty, just like me. I fell in love with Arthur Lee, and that was the dumbest thing I've ever done in my whole life, because he ain't a bit of damn good. Don't you make the same mistake, Chrissy. Don't ever fall in love."

"Okay."

She hugged me again. "I know you don't really understand all of this, but one day you will, and you'll thank me."

I nodded as I leaned into the hug.

I never forgot what she said, what she taught me. There were more lessons, too. Lessons about men and how a woman should carry herself, and how to survive. She'd take me and Kenny Ray on long walks through the woods and show us where to pick big, juicy muscadines or poke salad or how to suck the sweetness from a honeysuckle plant. She showed me how to make a path to keep from getting lost. So many lessons. I loved Aunt Joyce. To me, she was the smartest woman in the world. She taught me more than a school ever would.

***

Boom! Boom! Boom!

I sat up on the pallet, my heart racing at the sound of someone beating on Grandma Orene's front door. Kenny Ray started to cry. Grandma Orene jumped out of bed in her night gown. "Who in the name of Jesus is it?!" she yelled.

Boom! Boom! Boom! "It's the sheriff! Open this door!"

Grandma Orene snatched on her robe and quickly waddled to the front door while I sat on the pallet hugging Kenny Ray and trying to quiet him down.

I heard the front door open and then I heard her say, "Sheriff? You ain't the sheriff."

"You sassing me, nigger?!"

The next thing I heard was a loud thud, and then Aunt Joyce screamed, "Mama! What kind of man are you that you'd hit an old woman?!" I didn't even know Aunt Joyce was awake, but it would've been impossible for her to sleep through that commotion.

I stood from the pallet and stepped into the hallway with Kenny Ray holding onto me. I inched my way to the living room doorway and saw the men. There were five or six of them—white men. The one doing the talking was big and tall and extremely pale. He had dirty blond hair and a shaggy beard. And he was ugly. My eyes shifted to Grandma Orene who was sitting on the floor holding her head. There was blood oozing between her fingers. Aunt Joyce fell to her knees beside Grandma Orene. "You all right, Mama?"

Grandma Orene nodded slightly. "Yeah, I'm okay." She looked up at the men. "What's going on, sir? We... we ain't done nothing. Ain't none of us done nothing in here, sir."

"There's a fellow lives here. We looking for him," the man said.

"My son? He's not here. What y'all need wit' him?"

The man's eyes narrowed as he stared down at Grandma Orene. "Someone robbed the old Johnson store. Witness said it was a Negro man. We bringing in all the Negro men around these parts for questioning. Now, where is he?"

"What Negro man be stupid enough to rob a white store?" Aunt Joyce asked.

Grandma Orene shot her a look and then said, "Sir, I don't know where my son is right now. He grown. But I can promise you that he ain't robbed no store."

"Mm-hmm, well, you tell him we looking for him." He lifted his bloodshot eyes and rested them on me. "Whose kids?"

Aunt Joyce sprang to her feet and rushed to me and Kenny Ray. "These my brother's kids. My *other* brother's kids. He up north."

The man's mouth spread into a brownish, chewing tobacco-tinged smile. "That sure is a pretty little girl. She's gonna make somebody real happy one day."

"She's just a little girl, you nasty old—"

The man stomped over to Aunt Joyce and slapped her so hard, she fell to the floor.

"Joyce!" Grandma Orene shrieked.

"You better learn some respect, nigger!" the man shouted at Aunt Joyce.

"Things are changing! You might get away with treating us like this

24

right now, but one day this mess you're doing is gonna get you in a lot of trouble! One day, we gon' be able to fight back!"

He smiled again, slowly walked over to Grandma Orene, and spat a mouthful of tobacco juice right on top of her head. Then he and all of the other men laughed as they left.

4

"Runnin'"

Uncle Larry had been missing for more than a week before his body turned up on the side of a dirt road deep in the woods. He'd been beaten so badly, you could barely tell it was him, but Grandma Orene recognized him the moment she saw his bloated body. The night he left, the same night those white men came looking for him, he never returned home. Grandma Orene had hoped and prayed he was somewhere with some woman and when the truth of what happened hit her, she was so devastated that she climbed into her bed and didn't leave it until Uncle Larry's funeral a week later. And even after he was laid to rest, she wasn't the same.

Nothing at her home was the same, either. She still cooked and cleaned, she still hummed, but there was a sadness that surrounded her. There was no more joy in her eyes, her smile had disappeared and was replaced by a look of pure sorrow. There were no more hugs for me and Kenny Ray, either. Meals were eaten in silence. She even stopped going to church. But who could blame her? Her son wasn't arrested.

There was no trial. He was murdered in cold blood and no one bothered to even find out who did it. An innocent man was dead, and no one cared.

Aunt Joyce changed, too. She spent most of her time closed off in her room, and when she did come out, she smelled and her hair was stuck to her head. She would mumble to herself, say stuff that didn't make any sense. As a matter of fact, the only thing she said that *did* make sense were words she repeated over and over again, "It's my fault he's dead. I shouldn't have sassed that white man… It's my fault he's dead…"

No one read to us anymore. No one talked to us, either. And for the first time in a long time, I kind of actually missed my mother. I wished she'd come and get us because being yelled at was better than being ignored.

A month after Uncle Larry's funeral, my wish sort of came true. My mother showed up out of the blue. I was sitting on the porch watching Kenny Ray play in the mud when a long blue car pulled into Grandma Orene's yard. I saw a white man sitting behind the wheel and a white woman in the passenger seat. I stood and rushed over to Kenny Ray, pulling him onto the porch with me. By then, the presence of white people meant trouble to me. I watched as the woman climbed out of the car with a big red smile on her face. She was wearing a green dress with a matching pillbox hat. She walked over to us, her gait unsteady as the muddy yard swallowed the heels of her green pumps. She stopped at the foot of the porch and opened her arms.

"My sweet babies! Look how you've grown! One would think it'd been a year instead of six months!!"

I looked down at Kenny Ray who broke from my grip and ran to her. "Mama!" he screamed.

She looked up at me. "Well, Chrissy. Come on here and give me a hug. I got some good news."

"You found Daddy?" I asked, though I wasn't really sure if that would be good news.

"No, but I got you a new daddy," she said as she glanced back at the white man in the car. "I got married!"

I just stood there and stared at her as the wind whipped through my hair. I had wished for her to come back, but now that she was there with some strange man, I wasn't quite sure how I felt about her. Had I really missed her, or was I just so desperate for something close to normal that I'd made myself miss her? As she smiled and cried and held Kenny Ray in her arms, I ran down the front steps and into the woods that surrounded my grandmother's house. Instinctively, I knew she was going to take us away. And I believed that if she did, I'd never see my grandmother and aunt again. And as bad as things had been since my uncle was killed, they were still better than they were after my daddy left, before she left us here.

I ran deeper and deeper into the woods. I wasn't sure where I was going, but after running for just a little while, my mother's voice faded and I couldn't hear her calling my name anymore. I ran until I was sure they couldn't find me, and then I stopped. I looked around at the tall trees surrounding me as I caught my breath. I felt so small out there, smaller than I really was. It was like I was an ant standing among giants. I sat down on the ground and hugged myself. I wasn't scared to be alone out there. I was more afraid of being found than anything.

I sat there for so long that the shadows cast by the trees began to fade as the sun set. I had planned to spend the night out there and then go back to my grandmother's house in the morning. Hopefully, my mother would be gone by then. The only thing I was really worried about was whether or not she'd still take Kenny Ray with her if she left without me. I didn't want him to go, either. But I'd rather he go than me. She was always a little nicer to him. I never knew why, but she was meaner to me. And I hated her because of it.

I heard a sound and turned to see where it came from, hoping that it wasn't my mother. *Oh, please don't let it be her,* I thought.

Well, it wasn't her. It was a man. A big man holding a shotgun—the man who'd come into my grandmother's house and spit on her head.

My heart jumped in my little chest as I stood to my feet. I stared at the giant of a man and decided that I'd rather take my chances with my mother than with him. I moved to run away but he caught hold of my arm and snatched me back. He spat a mouthful of tobacco on the ground by my feet and said, "Where you going, pretty little girl?"

I looked at him for a second and then I screamed at the top of my lungs. He slapped me and I screamed again.

"Stop yelling before I give you something to yell about!" he shouted.

I frowned up at him. "Let me go! Let me go!"

He bent over until his face nearly touched mine. "Give me a kiss and I will."

"No!"

He picked me up and pressed his mouth to mine; his wiry beard and moustache scratched my skin. I guess instinct kicked in, because I bit him and I bit him *hard*. He yelped and dropped me on the ground. I struggled to my feet and ran away, not stopping until I was back at my grandmother's house.

My mother spanked me that night. She spanked me with one of my dead uncle's belts for running away. And just as I thought, she announced that she was there to take me and Kenny Ray back up north with her. I cried so hard that night when I went to bed, but not because of the spanking, though it did hurt and the belt left marks on my butt. I cried because deep inside of my young heart and mind, I knew life up north with my mother and whoever the man sitting in my grandmother's living room was, was going to be bad.

5

"Evil"

The sound of someone screaming woke me up the next morning. I jumped to my feet and ran into the living room where my mother was standing in the doorway screaming at the top of her lungs. Grandma Orene pushed her way through the doorway and stepped onto the porch and then she started screaming, too. I watched her run into the yard and my mother run after her, and that's when I realized Aunt Joyce hadn't come out of her room. Even as confused as she could get sometimes since Uncle Larry was killed, there was no way she could've ignored all of that screaming. I ran to her room and pushed the door open only to find her bed empty, and that's when my little heart began to race. I walked back into the living room and this time, my mama's old, gray-haired husband, whose name she said was Henry, was standing in the doorway staring outside. Kenny Ray was standing behind him.

I was too scared to move a muscle, too scared to breathe, too. So I just stood there and held my breath until I heard my name called.

"Chrissy! Chrissy, bring us a sheet!" my mother said.

I walked into my grandmother's room, grabbed one of the many sheets she kept folded up on her dresser, and slowly made my way through the house, past Henry and my little brother, and outside onto the porch. There, from that vantage point, I saw a scene that I was never able to erase from my mind. Years later, after I was a grown woman with grandchildren, the sight of my aunt's badly beaten, bloody body lying naked in my grandmother's front yard still haunted me.

I stood there and stared as my grandmother cradled my aunt in her arms. I was scared to move. *Is she dead?* I wondered. I felt tears fill my eyes as I clutched that sheet and shook my head.

"Chrissy! Chrissy, come on! We need to cover her up," my mother said as she held Aunt Joyce's feet in her lap.

I eased down the steps and dragged myself to the center of the yard where they were. I held out the sheet and my mother grabbed it and began tucking it around Aunt Joyce's limp body. I moved backward as tears stained my cheeks. "She dead?" I asked.

"No, she just hurt is all. Just hurt," Grandma Orene said.

Aunt Joyce moaned as her swollen eyes fluttered open and stretched wide. "Don't … don't let him get me. Please! Make him stop! *Please!*"

"Ain't nobody gon' get you, baby. Mama's got you. Ain't gon' let nobody hurt you again," Grandma Orene whimpered.

Aunt Joyce wailed loudly and grasped onto her mother for dear life. She screamed and cried and writhed in her mother's arms and I just stood there and stared at her bruised face and neck, at the gashes in her chest, at the blood stains that were streaked down her legs. I stood there and wondered who could've been so evil that they'd hurt my aunt like that. They'd ruined her face, destroyed her beauty. And from the way she was screaming, they'd taken what was left of her mind.

"It was… it was that white man, the one who came here looking for Larry that time. The one with the beard," Aunt Joyce said. "He did this! He did this!"

I frowned as I remembered running into him in the woods the day before. Did he hurt Aunt Joyce because of me?

"He… he saw me sitting on the porch last night, grabbed me and dragged me into the woods, covered my mouth so I couldn't scream. And he…"

"Shh, baby. You don't have to talk no more. Let's get you in the house," Grandma Orene said.

"No! I gotta say this. He beat me and he raped me, and he said he'll be back. He said he's coming back for Chrissy."

6

"Mom"

Milwaukee—1966

Most people think that segregation and racism only existed in the south. That's not entirely true. While it might have been more volatile and more prevalent in the south, it existed everywhere in the United States—always had and probably always will in some way, shape, or form. Racism definitely existed in Milwaukee. So did classism and every other type of ism. I didn't like being there and being stared at, but I guess a white couple walking around with two black kids in the sixties was an odd sight to see, even if me and Kenny Ray were mixed. But at the time, I was just a little girl and being stared at made me feel like something was wrong with me.

My mother acted as if it didn't bother her at first, but soon Henry started complaining about how people were starting to treat him differently and refusing to hire him (he was a lawyer). Racial tensions were rising and blacks were taking to the streets in protest of what was going on in the United States. Protests and boycotts had become commonplace. They were tired of unfair housing practices and segregation and in Milwaukee, like so many other places, they were fighting back. Watching the news back then, I would remember Aunt Joyce's words to those white men who came into Grandma Orene's house and wonder if she knew that blacks were fighting for change.

At any rate, Henry was a man of prominence and being a black-sympathizer was bad for business, so he and Mama came up with the idea to take me out of school after I'd only been in there for a month, and make me and Kenny Ray stay at home all the time. That way, they wouldn't be throwing her half-Negro children into the faces of his important clients. After all, she was a teacher and she could teach me just as well as the teachers at school could—at least that was what she said, although that had never motivated her to teach us before. But when I say all the time, I mean *all the time*—day and night. No playing outside, no stepping onto the front stoop for fresh air. Nothing. I don't think I need to explain what that can do to a child. For one thing, it's just unhealthy for a child to never get any sunlight, and being young and full of energy and closed up like that could drive the best child to misbehave.

But I obeyed and tried to tell myself that at least we had nice clothes and plenty of food unlike when we lived with our mother before. And the house was huge with an upstairs, and it was so clean with shiny new furniture, and me and Kenny got to share a soft bed in our own bedroom. But even with those benefits, I never forgot how mean our mother could be—another reason I obeyed. Kenny Ray, on the other hand, had a selective memory. He only remembered the good things about our mother, like the hugs and kisses she would give us when she was in a good mood. He seemed to have forgotten how she'd yell at us for nothing or whoop us out of her own frustration. But I never forgot, and if it hadn't been for what that white man told Aunt Joyce about me, I would've left Grandma Orene's house kicking and screaming. But I was scared of that man. As a matter of fact, I was more afraid of him than I'd ever been of my mother.

One day, about a week into our house arrest, Kenny Ray climbed into my mother's lap and said, "I like our new daddy. He nice."

I was sitting on the floor playing with a doll and in my young mind, I was hoping Kenny Ray wouldn't say anything to upset her. I could already tell she was tired of us being around her so much. She didn't work, so she spent all of her days in the house, too, "teaching us." What he'd said was sweet, but she had a way of twisting things sometimes.

"He's just the cat's pajamas, isn't he, peanut?" She gave Kenny Ray a little tap on the cheek.

I relaxed a little. She only called him peanut when she was in a good mood.

"What that mean?" Kenny Ray asked.

"That means he's an excellent man."

"Oh," he said, sounding confused. I was sure he had no idea what excellent meant, either.

She turned her attention to me. "Chrissy, put that doll up and write your letters for me."

I sighed quietly. I knew my letters like I knew the back of my hand. I was way past learning the alphabet. Thanks to Aunt Joyce, I could even read a little. I would've rather been reading than writing those doggone letters again. I guess my frustration showed on my face, because by the time I made it over to the dining room table and had picked up the pencil, she was standing next to me, wagging her finger in my face.

"Don't you take that attitude with me, little girl! I could've left you back at Orene's! You wanna go back to Orene's? Take your chance with that man who hurt Joyce?"

"I ain't got no attitude," I said softly as I sat in the chair and began to scribble the letters onto the paper—*Aa… Bb… Cc…*.

Mama kneeled next to the chair and brought her face close to mine. "What did you say?"

I glanced at her, saw the fire in her eyes, and said, "Nothin'."

"You *did* say something, Chrissy."

I shook my head. "No, I didn't."

"She said she ain't got no attitude," Kenny Ray said from his seat on the floor where he was playing with one of his little toy cars.

Mama's head jerked around to face Kenny Ray and I knew one of us was about to get it. "I know what she said, Kenny Ray!" she yelled. I guess he wasn't her "peanut" anymore.

"Why you ask, then?" he said, his eyes all big and innocent.

I held my breath as she sprung to her feet, stomped over to him, and slapped him so hard it hurt *my* cheek. When he began to cry, she screamed at him to shut up, then she started yelling at me.

"Look what you made me do to your little brother! I swear, I should've killed you in my womb, Chrissy!"

I dropped my eyes, and did what I always did when she said stuff like that. "I'm sorry, Mama."

She scoffed. "You're sorry?" She walked over to me and poked my forehead, *hard.* Then she left the living room. A few seconds later, I heard her bedroom door slam shut and I could hear her crying loudly. I rubbed my forehead as I walked over to Kenny Ray and held him in my arms. I told him that everything would be okay. But I knew that was a lie. As long as we had to stay in that house with Mama, day after day, I knew things would only get worse.

***

That night, when they thought me and Kenny were asleep, I heard my mama and Mr. Henry talking. I heard her say how she was tired of being cooped up in the house with me and Kenny Ray every day. She said it was unfair, that our daddy had gotten off easy. Then I heard Mr. Henry say something that kept me from sleeping for the rest of the night.

"Well, sweetie, I highly doubt the man intended to get himself killed."

Killed? My daddy was dead?

"Well, he sure intended to gamble and whore around, didn't he? That's how he got himself killed, owing money to some loan shark, and where was he when they found him? In some whore's apartment across town. If he wasn't already dead, I'd find him and kill him myself for leaving me alone with these kids!"

"Honey, it's only been a week, and you're not alone. I'm here with you."

"No, you're not! You get to go off to work every day and here I am, stuck with them!"

"They're your children, sweetie, and I thought you wanted them with you."

"I did… but they are so much like him—especially Chrissy. I just… I don't know."

"When are you going to tell them about him, that he's dead?"

"I'm not; I can't. If I tell them, I'll have to tell Kenny's people, and I can't do that to his mother. She's already lost one son, and from what I hear, Joyce still hasn't recovered from what happened to her. No matter how things ended between me and Kenny, his mother was always kind to me. I won't be the one to break her heart."

"She'll find out sooner or later, and you'll have to tell the kids."

"I know, but I just can't right now."

"Okay, sweetie. Look, why don't you put Chrissy back in school? That should give you some peace."

"But you said—"

"I know, but she needs to be in school and you need a break. You can take her to one of the more colored schools across town. I'll even get you a car just for that. That way, you don't have to be seen walking around the neighborhood with her."

"Oh, Henry, really?!"

"Yes."

I lay awake for the rest of that night, my little heart aching for my father and at the same time, leaping at the thought of going back to school.

7

"Inner City Blues (Make Me Wanna Holler)"

I was a whole grade behind because of not starting school on time in Arkansas, but I didn't care. I was just happy to be able to learn, *really* learn. And I was happy to be able to be away from my mother, too. I didn't really worry about Kenny Ray since, as I said before, my mother favored him to me and most of the anger she directed toward him was a result of something I said or did.

So every day, I put on a sailor dress or some other dress that Mama bought for me with Mr. Henry's money and a shiny pair of shoes—Mary Janes or saddle shoes—and with a matching ribbon in my curly hair, I rode to school in my mother's brand new car. I would barely give her a chance to stop the car before I jumped out and ran to the school. She would yell goodbye and tell me she loved me. I never answered, because I never really believed she did love me. It was more like she tolerated me. And I didn't really love her, either. I just needed her.

The kids at school fell into three groups—the ones who hated me because my skin was too fair and my hair was too fine since I was the only mixed kid in a school full of brown faces, the ones who hated me because I was a fast learner and could already read a little, and the one or two who were nice to me and I counted as my friends. Some of the kids would call me stupid names, throw dirt at me on the playground, push me in the classroom, glare at me when I raised my hand to answer a question, but when they really tried to fight me, my friend, Annie, would help me. Annie was tall and skinny and almost as light-skinned as me. My other friend, Margaret, was too little to help, but she always played with me and Annie on the playground and ate lunch with us. They were my best friends, my only friends, and I used to beg my mother to let me visit their homes and play with them on weekends. She would always say no, that twice a day of driving to the "colored" side of town was enough for her. When I asked if they could come over to our house to play, she said, "You're lucky Henry is allowing you and Kenny Ray to live here. I'm not letting any more black kids in this house."

We'd been living with our mother and Mr. Henry for months before we were finally allowed to play outside again. By then, Kenny Ray was so pale he could've easily passed for white. It was winter, but we didn't care. We'd sit out on the stoop, blowing steam from our mouths, huddling close as we watched the people walk by. We would sit in the freezing cold for hours, just happy to be outside. Life in Milwaukee wasn't perfect, but Kenny and I were as happy as we could be in the situation and we had each other. That was more than enough for us.

***

My mother was a predictable woman. I knew that even at my young age. She would be happy for a while. She'd be nice, cook dinner, bake cookies, kiss me and Kenny Ray on the forehead, comb my hair and put little bows in it, call Kenny her peanut and me her princess. And then, most times without warning, she'd switch. Something, *anything*, would set her off and the next thing I knew, she'd be screaming, telling whoever she was mad at how stupid they were. If it was me or Kenny Ray, she'd tell us how she wished we'd never been born, how meeting and falling in love with a nigger, as she put it, had ruined her life. She'd call us names, refuse to feed us dinner, and if it was a really bad day, she'd hit us—sometimes with her hand and other times with whatever she could find. When she and my father were still together, he'd stop her sometimes, tell her she was being too hard on us. Then she'd turn on him and start yelling at him and hitting him. I always thought that was the real reason he left—he was tired of her and her craziness. And that was probably why he ended up with another woman and never tried to come back to us before he was killed. My mother had a problem, a bad mental problem.

The funny thing is, she never seemed to get angry at Mr. Henry, or at least I never heard her yell at him or saw her hit him. She was always all smiles around him. It was actually weird to see how nice she was to him. I'd never seen her like that with anyone else except Grandma Orene and Aunt Joyce, and I didn't really understand it. After all, she was supposed to love me and Kenny Ray and our daddy more than anyone in the world and when she was in her good moods, she even said as much. So I was always confused as to why she was meanest to the people she was supposed to love the most. And it also made me wonder if she loved Mr. Henry at all. I'd never seen them hug or kiss or heard them fighting in bed like she and my father did. They were strange together, like roommates or something. I didn't truly understand what was going on between them, but I was glad his presence made her behave since she was never mean to us around him. And I was glad to be safe for the most part.

8

"Departure"

1970

We'd been living with my mother and Mr. Henry for almost four years, and I'd become accustomed to the rhythm of life with them. I loved school and so did Kenny Ray. And once Mr. Henry knew I liked reading, he bought me lots of books. Reading kept me occupied and out of trouble. I avoided my mother's anger and tried to teach Kenny Ray to do the same thing. But he didn't listen too well and even though he was Mama's favorite, he often found himself on the wrong end of a butt whooping. He was just stubborn, I guess. Bull-headed like my mama always said my daddy was. Kenny Ray reminded me of something I'd heard Grandma Orene say about Uncle Larry: "A hard head makes a soft behind." Kenny Ray's head was definitely hard and his behind had to be soft and mushy from all of those butt whoopings he got!

Mr. Henry's mother got sick around Christmas that year and he left to go see about her. She lived in New York City and my mother really wanted to go with him, said she'd always dreamed of going there and seeing a show on Broadway. Mr. Henry told her it would be too hard on his mother for me and Kenny Ray to come, too, and since she had no one around to keep us, she ended up having to stay in Milwaukee. From the moment I knew she would have to stay because of us, I knew Kenny Ray and I were going to get it. And I was right. She was in a bad mood from the second she dropped Mr. Henry off at the airport. She came home that day slamming doors and cussing under her breath, glaring at me and Kenny Ray. Told us to go to our room and not come out until she said so.

I did what she said, even stayed there through dinnertime though my stomach felt like it was eating itself. I had to pee really bad, too, but I held it. Kenny Ray couldn't hold his, so I let him use it in a cup that was in our room. When I could finally hold my pee no longer, I used it in a little toy bucket. We went to bed hungry that evening, but as the night wore on, my stomach started hurting so bad that it actually woke me up out of my sleep. I lay there for a long time in our dark room next to Kenny Ray, listening to him sleep and trying to listen for any signs of my mother still being awake. I knew it was late, but I had no idea what time it was and she had been known to stay up all night when she was mad like this. Sometimes, if she was really wound up, she would stay awake for days at a time, but she hadn't done anything like that since we'd been in Milwaukee.

After a while, I just couldn't take the pain anymore so I quietly climbed out of bed and tiptoed to the door. I slowly opened it, listened, and heard nothing, so I crept into the hallway and eased past my mother's bedroom door. I went into the kitchen, grabbed an apple off the table, and crept back toward my room. I was in the hallway next to my mother's door when I heard the sounds. Something was going on behind her closed door and it sounded like what she and my father used to do in their bed back in Arkansas and what I heard my Aunt Joyce doing that day in Grandma Orene's house. I stood there for a moment, confused, wondering if Mr. Henry was back and if he was, why they were making noises together that they'd never made before. I was still standing there when the noises stopped and the door swung open. It was a man who I'd never seen who'd opened the door. He was tall and dark brown like my father… and he was naked. My mother, who was naked, too, and sitting on the side of the bed, screamed at me to go back to my room. I ran to the room and slammed the door, waking Kenny Ray in the process. By then I knew something was wrong with this situation, and from the look in my mother's eyes, I knew I was about to be punished something awful. I fell to the floor behind the door and cried. Kenny Ray sat on the floor next to me and kept asking me what was wrong, but I couldn't answer him. I couldn't do anything but cry.

I'm not sure how long I laid there with my face on the floor, but it seemed like a long time before Mama stormed into the room, hitting me with the door. I sat up and watched through teary eyes as she dragged Kenny Ray back to our bed and yelled at him to go back to sleep. He ducked under the covers and whimpered softly. My eyes followed my mother as she slowly made her way over to me. Even in the darkness of that bedroom, I could see the anger etched across her pale face and it scared me to death. Instinct told me to run, but I was too afraid of the punishment I knew she'd hand down whenever she caught me. So I just sat there and waited for her to do whatever she was going to do. I would take my whooping and just go to sleep and pretend it never happened, and maybe she would be in a better mood in the morning.

Once she reached me, she grabbed me by the hair and pulled me to my feet. "Ouch!" I wailed.

"Shut up!" she screamed. Kenny's whimpers grew louder as she dragged me from my room to hers and shut the door behind us. She released my hair and pushed me onto the bed, and then she paced the room for a long time. I mean a *really* long time, so long that I almost asked her to just whoop me and get it over with. All of the waiting was worse than anything. When she finally stopped pacing, she stood there and stared at me for a minute, and then she said, "I deserve to be happy, don't I?

I just sat there. She was looking at me, but she was kind of looking through me, too, so I really wasn't sure if I should answer her.

"I deserve to be happy. I mean, I'm happy with Henry, but he can't take care of some of my needs and Robert, well, *he* certainly can."

I assumed Robert was the man I saw coming out of her bedroom, but I didn't ask. I merely watched as she sat beside me on the bed.

She turned and fixed her green eyes on mine. "I know you don't understand what I'm talking about right now, but one day you will. You'll understand why Robert was here, why I needed him to be here, and why I need Henry, too. Henry's good to me, took my Negro children in and everything," she said as if she was talking to someone other than one of her Negro children.

I kept my mouth shut and glanced at the belt that hung on the bedpost, hoping that maybe she'd keep talking and this one time, I would avoid feeling the sting of the thick leather.

"I love Henry, I really do. And I love Robert, too. I—" She stopped and looked at me as if just realizing who I was. "You're gonna tell Henry about Robert, aren't you? I know you are."

I frowned slightly and shook my head. It hadn't even occurred to me that what happened was something to tell anyone. "No, ma'am. I'm not."

She stood from the bed, reached for the belt. "Yes, you are! You're going to tell and ruin everything for me! Your daddy deserted us and left us to starve to death and I find us a nice white man to take care of us and you are going to ruin it!" Her words came out in such a rush, I could barely understand what she was saying.

"No! No, I won't! I won't tell nothing!"

She lifted the belt and I covered my head with my hands knowing that when she started swinging, she didn't care where the strap landed. The belt slapped against the forearm I was using to protect my face. I'd been on the wrong end of that belt enough times to know what a belt to the face felt like, and it did not feel good at all. The belt to the arm hurt, but had it hit my face, it would've been ten times worse. I heard her mumble something and then she hit my leg. My first instinct was to grab the spot on my bare leg where I was sure a welt was forming, but I was familiar with this part of the game, too. She'd hit my leg hoping I'd uncover my face because she loved hitting my face, mostly because, despite my being half black, I was accustomed to hearing three little words I doubted my mother had ever heard: *you're so pretty*. I heard it all the time, from white folks and black folks alike. Some people admired me for my looks, others despised me because of them. My mother belonged in the latter group.

I squeezed my eyes shut in anticipation of the next blow and... *nothing*. The room was quiet except for my own huffing and sniffling. When I finally opened my eyes, my mother was staring at me with a calm expression on her face.

"Go back to bed," she said. "I know what I'm gonna do about you."

I was afraid to move. What if this was a trick? What if the moment I let my guard down, she tore into me with the belt again?

"Go *now*!" she shrieked. I bolted from the bed and sprinted out the door to my room. I slammed my bedroom door, huddled close to a sleeping Kenny Ray, and cried myself to sleep.

***

A few days later, Mama woke us up early in the morning and threw a couple of suitcases on the floor. "Pack up. We're leaving. And hurry! I want to get this done before Henry gets back next week."

I had no idea what she was talking about or where we were going, but Kenny and I obeyed her, knowing it was best we did. Otherwise we'd get the belt, and no one wanted the belt that early in the morning. So we packed, washed up, dressed, and all three of us piled into Mama's Ford. Soon we were heading out of Milwaukee. When Kenny Ray asked a question I'd been wanting to ask but was too afraid to actually voice, I stared at Mama's reflection in the rearview mirror, anxiously awaiting her answer.

"Where we going, Mama?" he asked.

"Back to Arkansas," she answered.

As images of the man with the beard filled my mind, I swallowed hard, held back tears, and stared out at the highway.

9

"Sad Tomorrows"

My stomach did flip flops the entire trip from Wisconsin to Arkansas, and when I wasn't thinking about the man with the beard and the evil look that always seemed to be in his eyes, I was thinking about what he did to Aunt Joyce, what he said he'd do to me. When Mama stopped to get us something to eat, I told her I wasn't hungry. When she stopped so that we could use the restroom, I vomited. When she told us to close our eyes and take a nap, I closed mine, but wouldn't let myself fall asleep because I knew my dreams would be nightmares of *him*.

It was dark when we passed the sign that announced our entry into Lonoke County, Arkansas. My eyes were glued to the window; a mixture of anticipation and despair washed over me. It would be good to see my grandmother and aunt again. They had been kind to us and I missed them. But then there was the threat of the man, of what he might do to me. I was older, but I was still small, skinny, and young—a little girl who would be no match for a man as tall and big as him. As I stared at the trees that lined the two-lane highway, I tried to rationalize that maybe if I just stayed in the house all the time, I'd be safe. Maybe no one would know I was there and if no one knew I was there, maybe he wouldn't come for me. Then I remembered what it had been like during the time when Kenny and I weren't allowed to leave the house in Milwaukee and I knew I never wanted to live like that again, closed up in a stuffy house, no sunlight. No, I didn't want to go through that again at all.

I closed my eyes for a second and prayed the way I remembered Grandma Orene would do sometimes. I prayed that the man had moved away or was dead or that he was different, better, and didn't hurt people anymore. It was the first time I'd prayed in my life, and I hoped that God could or would hear me. I hoped he knew who I was.

When I felt the car stop, I opened my eyes and was surprised to see we weren't parked in front of the house I had grown to love those years ago. This was a smaller house and it was run down. As a matter of fact, it reminded me of my Mama's and Daddy's house. I sat up straight, rubbed my eyes, looked at the house again and realized it *was* the same house, but somehow, it looked bigger, like someone had added rooms to it or something.

Had Grandma Orene moved into our old house? I told myself that was crazy. Why in the world would she leave her big house for this little shack?

"Y'all awake?" Mama asked.

I nudged a sleeping Kenny Ray and said, "Yes, ma'am."

"Get on out, then."

Kenny rubbed his eyes and hopped out of the backseat behind me. "Where we at?" he asked.

"Looks like our old house," I answered.

Mama smiled as she reached for Kenny's hand. "It is. My brother and his family live here now. Looks like he fixed the place up some." She sounded so happy, a stark contrast even to how she'd sounded when she told us to get out of the car. I guess she was just that happy to be rid of us, or at least of me.

She walked us up the unsteady steps of the wooden house and knocked on the screen door which hung crooked from its hinges. We stood there for a few minutes before the front door squealed open to reveal a short, very unattractive, thin white woman with dark eyes and hair.

"Tabitha!" our mother shrieked. "It is so good to see you! I'm so glad you and Teddy can keep the kids for a while. This is Kenny and this is Chrissy," she said, resting a hand on top of each of our heads. She peeped around Tabitha and added, "Is Teddy home?"

The woman didn't answer. She just chewed on something that was in her mouth, swung the door open wider, and stepped back so that we could walk into the house, our old house. The tiny living room held a different sofa and an easy chair, both of which were covered with tattered, dingy quilts. The wooden floor was dirty with muddy boot tracks visible in several places. The place smelled of burnt wood and must. Standing in a doorway which led to what used to be me and Kenny's room were two pale children, a boy and a girl.

"Are these your kids?" Mama asked. "The last time I saw them, they were just babies!"

Tabitha nodded. "This here's Carrie and Toby. They're ten and nine now."

"Chrissy's ten, too!" Mama practically yelled. She was really putting on an act for this woman.

I frowned slightly as the two kids stared at me and Kenny. Finally, the boy said, "They niggers." His southern accent was so thick, I wondered if there was something wrong with his tongue.

Tabitha grabbed a tin can from the floor, spit what looked like tobacco juice into it, and wiped her mouth with the sleeve of her thin, faded blue dress. "They is half niggers," she corrected.

I looked up at Mama who was still wearing a fake smile as if their words hadn't fazed her.

Tabitha reached into a sagging pocket on the front of her dress, pulled out a pouch, stuck a plug of tobacco in her cheek, and said, "Y'all go tell your daddy Aunt Patty is here with her kids."

The kids turned almost in unison and ran deeper into the house.

While we waited for them to return with their daddy, Tabitha just stood there and stared at us as she chewed her tobacco. Mama kept smiling and smoothing her hands over me and Kenny's heads. I could tell she was nervous and anxious. So was I. In the few short minutes since we'd arrived in that house, I knew this wasn't any place I wanted to be in for long.

When they made it back, the girl said, "He comin'." And then the two of them stood against the wall this time and resumed staring at us.

I wished I could run away from there, but where could I go? My own mother didn't want me, it probably wasn't safe to live with Grandma Orene, and I didn't know what condition she and Aunt Joyce were in anyway. Maybe they were still sad about Uncle Larry. Maybe they were both dead. Maybe the man with the beard had—

A man appeared, one I recognized as the man who came to Grandma Orene's house those years ago to check on us. My mother's brother. As the man walked into the room, the kids scampered over to their mother and all three of them quickly left the room as if they were afraid to be in his presence. I could see why, though, because his eyes were so strange-looking, almost emotionless, as he stepped toward us. Kenny ducked behind Mama. I lowered my eyes from his face.

"These them, huh?" he asked.

"Yes, these are my babies—Kenny Jr. and Chrissy."

I looked up to see him nod. "Humph, done grown since I saw them over at Kenny's mama's house."

"Yes, they have. I really do thank you for keeping them for me just until I can figure things out."

He nodded again. "Can't blame your husband for not wanting to keep taking care of nigger kids. Don't know how long I'ma be able to do it. I don't like being around niggers much myself. You know that."

Mama began to twist her hands in front of her and I wondered why she'd lied to her brother. Her husband didn't have anything to do with us leaving. He probably didn't even know she was bringing us here.

"I know," was her response.

"I told you when you started up with that Kenny Ray Greene that wasn't nothing good gonna come of it."

"I know," she repeated.

"Everybody told you. Ma and Pa. *Everybody*. Now look at ya'. He done ran off and left you with these two mutts."

"It's not my fault he left, Teddy."

"Whose fault is it, then?" He smiled a grimy, brown-toothed smile that made my stomach turn and I quickly dropped my eyes again. "Oh, yeah," he said. "He couldn't find work around here."

Mama reached into her purse and pulled out some money. She shoved it toward him. "Here. This should help with food and all. I guess you'll have to figure out a way to get them to and from school. They're real smart. Chrissy reads well."

"They's a colored school down the road from the Parson farm now. They s'posed to be done integrated the schools here by now, but any nigger with good sense know not to try it."

Mama nodded. "Then they can walk to school. That's good."

We all stood in silence for a few minutes. I glanced back at Kenny, who looked like he was on the brink of tears, and tried to give him a reassuring smile, but I was afraid and sad, myself. Afraid of this man who looked at me like I was a rodent or a bug he wanted to smash, and sad because my mother thought it was okay to leave me and Kenny with him.

Finally, Mama turned around and kneeled in front us. "You two be good. You'll be fine here. Teddy is your uncle and his family is your family. This is your real home, anyway. This where me and your daddy made you, Kenny." She smiled at us and glanced at Teddy. He must've given her a look because the smile quickly faded. "I'll be back for you as soon as I can."

"You ain't gon' stay the night before hitting the road again? That's a long drive," he said.

She stood and smoothed the front of her skirt, glanced around at the room. "I'm going to check into a motel in Little Rock. I thought it'd be best to say goodbye to the kids now instead of tomorrow. Make it easier on them."

Uncle Teddy stepped closer to us and both Kenny and I scrambled away from him toward the broken-down sofa. He gave us a satisfied, lopsided grin as he reached for our mother, clutching her upper arm. "Okay, well, let me walk you out, sis."

Our mother merely nodded and let her brother lead her out to her car. I slowly walked to the open front door and watched them. Mama almost looked scared as she listened to him talk. I couldn't make out what he was saying, but I knew it was nothing good or nice. When he turned to come back into the house, I rushed back over to the sofa where Kenny was seated, seemingly glued to the cushion with tears in his eyes.

Uncle Teddy entered the house and slammed the door behind him. He moved in front of us and peered down at our frightened faces, his features darkened in the dim lighting of the room. "I don't much like niggers and I don't want you here, but your mama is my sister so I'm doing this for her." He crouched in front of us. "Now there's rules you need to follow, so listen real close…"

***

Hands, knees, and eyes on the floor. Hands, knees, and eyes on the floor.

Those words, words I'd heard over and over again, screamed in my head.

Hands, knees, and eyes on the floor.

Whack!

I knew the sound of Uncle Teddy's belt hitting flesh as well as I knew the sound of water running in the tub or pee streaming into a toilet. I knew it too well. And I knew that either one of my cousins or my brother had eyeballed him. We'd been on our knees for hours now, practicing the cardinal rules of my uncle's house:

1. Bow when he enters the room.
2. Stay in that position until he leaves the room.
3. Never, ever look him in the eye.

I was smart, so I hardly ever broke the rules. And anyway, if I didn't look at him, maybe he wouldn't see the hatred in my eyes. I hated him. I hated his home. I hated his weak wife and his evil children. I hated my mother for leaving me there. I hated my father for not taking me and Kenny with him when he left and for eventually getting himself killed. I hated everything and everyone.

"Kenny Ray! Your little half-black behind is gonna learn to follow my rules! Or else I'm gonna beat the rebellious nigger out of you!"

Whack!

I could hear Kenny whimpering. He knew not to cry out. He knew that would only make things worse. I squeezed my eyes tightly shut and willed myself not to look at my baby brother. Because if I looked at him, I knew I would have to do something to help him.

Whack!

"You hear me, Kenny Ray?! I told your damn mama to stop sneaking around with the hired help. But did she listen? No! Just kept right on sneaking 'round my ma and pa's farm with him. Hiding out in barns and letting him have his way with her and what did it get her? He's gone and she's stuck with you two mutts. Now she done left you two on me because her new husband don't want you. I let you into my house and how do you repay my kindness? By breaking my rules!"

Whack!

I gritted my teeth.

"I'm… I'm sorry, Uncle Teddy," Kenny Ray said softly.

"Did I say you could speak, nigger?!"

Whack!

I covered my ears with my hands, heard Uncle Teddy's feet shift on the weak floor.

"Hands, knees, and eyes, Chrissy!" he shouted, his attention on me now.

I quickly slapped my hands back onto the floor.

Whack!

The belt hit the small of my back and my knees buckled. I could hear soft snickering beside me. No doubt it was my cousin, Carrie.

Whack!

Now Carrie began to whimper. At least he was an equal opportunity abuser. His kids got as bad as me and Kenny Ray did. So did his wife if she got out of line, as he put it. I'd seen him hit her plenty of times— with his belt, with his fist, with whatever he could get ahold of. He didn't respect her any more than he did the rest of us. She didn't have to bow or do the other stuff us kids had to do, but she couldn't speak unless he told her to. There were certain ways she had to cook his dinner, she had to give him a bath after he got home from work at the lumber yard, stuff like that. Stuff Uncle Teddy called her "wifely duties."

We'd been living there with Uncle Teddy in our old house for almost a year. We knew the rules. We knew them well, but he still made us practice every Sunday. I wondered if this was his idea of church or something. He sure acted like he was our God, but from what I knew of God, he loved kids. Uncle Teddy acted like he hated them, or at least he acted like he hated the kids that lived in his house. Well, he didn't hate us any more than we hated him. At least I know *I* hated him. I hated him almost as much as I hated my mother for bringing me back to Arkansas to live with him. He was her brother; didn't she know what a horrible person he was? Didn't she realize he'd be mean to us?

Yeah, I hated her every single second of every day. I hated her every night when me and Kenny had to sleep on the hard living room floor in our own house because Uncle Teddy said he wasn't wasting his money on buying beds for niggers. I hated her when their old mangy dog got more food to eat at dinnertime than me and Kenny did. I hated her when we had to eat on the living room floor because Uncle Teddy didn't allow niggers at his table. I hated her when I had to wear my cousin, Carrie's, dingy hand-me-downs to school after I outgrew my clothes even though she was much bigger than me and her clothes bagged on me. I hated her when our cousins would tease Kenny relentlessly. I hated her when Kenny and I had to walk so far to school every day in the heat or cold. I hated her when I was teased at school because my hair was tangled or because my skin was light, or because I was skinny, or because I was smart. I hated her when Uncle Teddy would flash the money she sent us and tell us how he'd be damned if he spent it on a couple of mutts. I hated her when Kenny Ray would cry next to me at night and ask me when she was coming back to get us. I hated her when I lied to him and said soon.

She never called. She never called even once after she dropped us off. Just sent money to Uncle Teddy with notes asking how we were.

What kind of mother just takes her kids to another state to live with a racist and for a whole year not call or come back to check on them? No birthday gifts or Christmas gifts or nothing. And all because she didn't want her husband to find out she was cheating? No kind, that's what kind. I vowed that if I ever had kids, I'd be a better mother than her, knowing that that wouldn't be hard to do at all. As long as I kept them with me, I'd already be doing better than her.

10

"Remember the Children"

1971

The summer was almost unbearable. It wasn't just the stifling, unrelenting heat or the flies that seemed to multiply by the second or the smell of the chicken coop behind the house or the fact that we were made to stay outside all day. It was knowing that the next day would bring more of the same. There was no school to break up the torture of being there and being treated less than human in our parents' own house. The walk to and from school was long, but I made the most of the fact that it kept me away from the house and away from Uncle Teddy even longer. It kept me off of my knees for hours at a time, staring at a floor whose grooves, cracks, and tiny dirt tracks I'd memorized, while he sat and watched TV in what amounted to me and Kenny's bedroom. But in the summer, when there was no school, there was nothing to do but try to play outside and try to forget that life could be better, because thinking of life before this—life with Grandma Orene or at Mr. Henry's house—would only make things worse since it didn't look like we were ever going to be able to leave this place, as our mother had obviously abandoned us for good.

I felt worse for Kenny than I did for myself. He was younger and weaker than me and while Mama had favored him, it seemed Uncle Teddy hated him even more than he did me. Kenny's skin was slightly darker than mine since we'd both gotten our color back from our temporary Wisconsin house arrest years earlier, and he looked more like our father than I did, and Uncle Teddy never let him forget it. "You look just like your nigger Daddy," he'd say when he decided to be mad at Kenny for no reason. I think it would've been better or a little more understandable if he were drunk when he went on those rants or when he flew into rages, but he never drank, just chewed tobacco. He was naturally mean and hateful and it was almost too much for Kenny. At one point during that first summer, Kenny stopped talking almost completely. No matter what I said or did, I couldn't get him to talk to me. He just walked around with his shoulders sagging and his eyes glued to the ground. Most days, he'd find a tree to sit under and draw circles in the dirt with a stick. He never played, barely ate. By the end of the summer, he was so skinny that Uncle Teddy even noticed and started screaming at him to eat more, even told Aunt Tabitha to put more food on his plate.

That first summer seemed to crawl by, too. The days were so long I started to wonder if time was slowing down or something. But I guess when you're miserable and hot, time is a little distorted. Anyway, that was how we spent our first summer with Uncle Teddy—hot and miserable. I had never prayed so hard in my life as I did then for school to start back up.

***

One hot, late August afternoon, Kenny and our cousins and I were playing in the woods right behind the house when we heard a car pull up—well, they never really played with me and Kenny, it was more like they played in the same vicinity as us. We all took off to see who it was, because we knew it wasn't Uncle Teddy. He drove a loud pickup that you could hear from a mile away. There was no mistaking when he made it home. No, we knew this was another car and for some reason, we all seemed equally excited about having company though we were all grimy and sweaty from having been outdoors the balance of the day. I guess it was because we rarely had company. Uncle Teddy said it was because no self-respecting white person wanted to visit someone who was housing niggers.

We raced from the partial shade of the woods to the front of the old house, sweat seeming to multiply with each step. When I saw the car, I halted, not sure what to think or if I could really believe what I was seeing. Was it really possible that after all that time, more than a year, she was there?

Kenny never stopped running until he ran right into her, throwing his arms around her and uttering the first word I'd heard come from his mouth in weeks, "Mama!"

I stood there, inches from the car, my eyes glued to her as Kenny hugged her waist tightly, unsure of how to feel, what to feel. A part of me was happy. I can admit that. A part of me was deliriously happy and relieved and hopeful that the torture of being there in that horrible place with a horrible man and his weak wife was nearly over. Then again, I was angry, angry that she was there. Angry that it took so long for her to come back. Then another part was skeptical that any good would come of her being there. She was a liar and a mean woman. What if she was just there to tell more lies, to hurt us again? Regardless of the mixture of feelings I was experiencing, hatred was foremost in my mind. As she stood there in a pretty, bright yellow sundress with a smile on her face, I absolutely despised her.

She rubbed her hand across Kenny's head and said, "You've gotten so tall—tall and skinny." She looked up at me. "You're both skinny. You'd think my brother wasn't feeding you."

I gave her a sneer. "He barely is."

My mother frowned and her eyes quickly dropped back to Kenny. She kissed the top of his head. "Oh, goodness! You need your hair washed!"

I crossed my skinny arms over my skinny chest and continued to stare at her. I wondered if she noticed the shabby, ill-fitting clothes we wore, too. Did she notice how dry and brittle my hair was? Could she smell me from where I stood?

She lifted her eyes to meet mine again and said, "Well, Chrissy? Can I have a hug?"

Something about the sweetness of her voice made me even angrier. Couldn't she see in my eyes how mad I was, how hurt I was? Maybe she saw it and just didn't care. Well, if she didn't care, neither did I. So I just stood there with my eyes glued to her.

"Chrissy?" she repeated.

I shifted my feet, tightened my arms across my chest. I wanted to walk over to her and spit in her pale, pasty face. I wanted to knock her to the ground and cover her pretty yellow Wisconsin dress in red Arkansas clay dirt. I wanted to scream and yell at her until my throat hurt, until I was out of breath, until I ran out of words to say to her.

"Well, that's okay. Maybe later. I guess you're surprised to see me. I'll only be here for a couple of days so I hope you feel like giving me a hug soon."

My stomach dropped, although I'm not sure why. I had expected as much. Actually, it would've been a shock if she'd said she'd come to take us back home. But I suppose hearing her say it, even after she'd seen with her own two eyes the condition me and Kenny were in, was still a bit of a surprise to me. The thought of it all—her not caring enough to rescue us, me hating her too much to want to go with her but wanting to be taken away from that place at the same time, the subsequent heartbreak I knew was ahead for Kenny—was too much for me. Before I knew it, I was on my knees, right there in the dusty front yard, heaving up my lunch of a bologna sandwich and water. As my body spasmed, I felt a hand on my back, heard my mother's panicked voice. I stumbled to my feet and snatched away from her. "Don't touch me!"

"I just want to make sure you're all right, sweetie. Let me help you!"

Through blurry, tear-filled eyes, I looked at her and began swinging my arms wildly. My fist connected with her jaw as I yelled, "Get away from me! Get away from me! I hate you!"

"Chrissy! Chrissy, stop!" my mother squawked.

My eyes were so full of tears that my vision was all but gone. I felt as if I were looking at the world through a jar full of murky water. I continued to swing and yell, making so much commotion that I didn't hear Uncle Teddy's old truck pull up. I didn't hear the thud of his boots as he strode across the yard. But I felt his hand tightly grasp my arm. I heard his gruff voice as he yelled something I couldn't make out. And I felt the palm of his hand as it seared my cheek.

After he hit me, he released my arm and let me tumble to the ground. I looked up to see my mother standing there with a look of horror on her face and I hated her even more.

11

"Reasons"

2012

Sometimes I wonder why I write this stuff down.

I mean, other than to get it out of my head, why do I *really* write it?

Who do I expect to read it? My daughters, one of which is lost to me physically, the other in hatred? I was a bad mother, probably one of the worst. I know that and I regret it, but my bad was the best I could do. I wish I could've been better for them and to them. Maybe I started writing my story so they could understand why I was what I was. But do I really want them to read this? Do I really want them to know?

12

"You Went Away"

August 1971

My mother's presence had no bearing on how her brother treated us and his rules still applied. We still were not allowed to eat at the table with his family. My mother was, but her Negro children were not. Our portions of the night's meal were still meager, and when it was time for bed, we were still made to sleep on an old quilt with a tattered blanket covering us. The little house was still hot and stuffy as we settled into a slumber with our stomachs growling.

Late that night I was awakened by the voices of my mother, who was supposed to be asleep on the couch, and Uncle Teddy. I kept my eyes closed as their voices, angry voices, filled my ears. Kenny was still fast asleep.

"What are you doing with the money I send?" my mother hissed. "They are rail thin and those clothes look like you found them on the side of the road somewhere. You better not be mistreating my kids, Teddy!"

"Have you lost your mind, girl? Who the hell do you think you're talking to like that? I ain't that nigger you let knock you up and I ain't your nigger kids. You better get that straight before I remind you of exactly who the hell I am! You better be glad I let them mutts of yours stay in my home!"

"It was mine and Kenny Ray's home first!"

"No, it was my daddy's house, first. The daddy who hates niggers more than I do. The daddy who hasn't cared about you since the day you let Kenny knock you up. You better thank your maker I'm allowing those kids on my daddy's property. He didn't like it none too much when he found out!"

"He doesn't mind," she said, not at all sounding sure of her own words. "He let us stay here before."

"Because our mama begged him! After you left, he figured you were gone for good. Never thought you'd be back to leave these kids."

"What are you doing with my money, Teddy?" she repeated.

"Whatever the hell I want to! I'm owed that money for letting them stay here. You better be glad I ain't stomped a hole in both of 'em! You know I can't stand nig—"

"They're your kin, Teddy! I don't expect you to like them, but I do expect you to be kind to them!"

Then I heard a very familiar sound—the sound of flesh hitting flesh. I knew without opening my eyes that someone had been slapped and my mother's soft whimpers told me she had been on the receiving end and not Uncle Teddy.

"Now, I don't know what's done got into you up north other than probably another Negro man, but you know better than to talk to me like that. You should be on your damn hands and knees thanking me for letting your kids, your *shame*, eat and sleep under my roof. As a matter of fact, get on your knees right now and thank me!"

I slowly opened one eye, but I didn't move. I could see my mother holding one side of her face with her hand as she slowly slid from the chair onto her bony knees. The only thought in my head was that her pretty, silky blue nightgown was going to get dirty on that floor.

Down on her knees, her shoulders shook as she covered her mouth with her hands and cried; there was fear in her eyes. Uncle Teddy stood from the table and stared down at her. I almost felt sorry for her, but then I remembered that this was what Kenny and I faced every day. Uncle Teddy was a monster and from the looks of what was going on between them, he had always been a monster. And she knew it, and she still left us with him.

"That's better. That's where you belong anyway. Letting those black men touch you, use you. You don't ever deserve to walk upright. Hell, you need to *stay* on all fours. Get those hands on that floor!"

She dropped onto her hands and knees, whimpering the whole time. "Teddy, *please*. My kids are right over there. Don't do this right now. Don't make me…"

He shifted his eyes in me and Kenny's direction and I quickly shut my eye. Then I felt his footsteps as the floorboards slightly gave way under his weight. I felt him stand next to us, hoped and prayed he hadn't seen me with my eye open. I didn't feel like being on my knees.

"You know, Patty… for a half-breed, Chrissy is a pretty little girl. Prettier than you."

"I… I know. Teddy… Teddy, *please*," she replied through a sniffle.

His footsteps began again, this time in the opposite direction. I opened both eyes just a tad, and saw him reclaim his seat at the kitchen table.

"Get up," he said gruffly.

My mother scrambled to her feet and fell back into her seat. "Thank you, Teddy. Thank—"

"How much longer you expect me to house your kids, Patty?"

"I… I don't know. A few more months, maybe. Until I get things situated in Milwaukee. Then I'll be back for them."

"And the money?"

"I'll… I'll keep sending it. Do what you want with it. Just…"

"Just, *what?*"

"Nothing."

"I'ma need more."

"I don't know if I can get more."

"Then you better take them kids on back with you."

She sighed heavily. "I'll see what I can do."

He smiled a grimy-toothed smile and said, "I thought so."

I closed my eyes and fell back to sleep with more than hatred for my mother in my heart. I was disgusted by her weakness.

***

By the time Kenny and I woke up the next morning, our mother was already gone. One day, that was all she'd spent with us. Not even a whole day, really. And just like that, she was gone. No goodbye for me. No goodbye hug or kiss for Kenny Ray and he was the one who really needed and wanted a goodbye. She could've driven off the end of the earth for all I cared.

Something changed about my brother after Mama's visit. *He* changed. He was no longer just quiet and sad, he was angry, too, but not like me. Kenny's anger was quiet, secretive. I might have missed the transformation had I not seen it in his eyes—white hot anger like the fuse on a very unstable bomb. Almost instantly, I knew that eventually, he was going to get enough of our living situation, and of Uncle Teddy, and when that time came, he was going to blow and probably destroy anything and anyone in his path. He still wouldn't talk, but when he looked at everyone except me, you could see the cold hatred in his eyes. You could almost feel his rage. And a month or so after Mama's visit, I noticed that our cousins no longer teased him like they once had. They actually seemed a little afraid of him. So was I.

13

"Fantasy"

1972

Another school year began, Thanksgiving came and went, Christmas had long passed, it was almost summer again, and our mother still hadn't come back for us. She had said it would only be a few more months, but as usual, she'd lied. I had finally decided that we were never going to get to leave until maybe we were grown. So I tried to find ways to cope with living with Uncle Teddy. I immersed myself in books—books my teacher let me have, books I found in an old abandoned house deep in the woods, books I checked out from the library in town. I loved books, loved to read about other people's adventures or problems, or loves, or losses. Books kept my mind occupied and carried me far from the reality of my life.

When I would have to be on my hands and knees sometimes, I thought about the people in my books, the dashing hero and how he would swoop in and save me from the dragon—Uncle Teddy. When I sat on the hard floor to eat my little dinner, I imagined I was in a palace in France eating a four course meal. When Kenny would wake up crying from a nightmare (which he did almost every night after our mother's visit), I'd tell him about whichever book I was reading and the stories would lull him back to sleep. In a way, my love of reading saved both of us.

Evidently, Mama made good on her promise to send Uncle Teddy more money because around the end of May, he went out and bought himself a brand new pickup truck. He was so proud of that truck that the day he brought it home, he took us all for a ride in it. *Everyone*, including me and Kenny. Aunt Tabitha sat in the cab with Uncle Teddy while our cousins and us sat in the bed. That was one of the best days I could remember in a long time. Feeling the air hit my face, watching the trees and houses zip by, seeing dogs chase behind the truck, barking—it all felt so good and normal. Nothing had felt normal in a long time. I kind of wished it had been raining so that maybe the sorrow that seemed to cover every inch of me and Kenny could've been washed away.

He stopped and got us some hamburgers, fries, and shakes—me and Kenny included! I ate so fast, I almost got sick. I hadn't eaten anything so delicious in a long, long time, since the last time I ate Grandma Orene's cooking. I thought about her from time to time, wondered if she was even still alive. And Aunt Joyce, I wondered how she was. Was she still sad about what the man with the beard did to her? Did they know my daddy was dead? Sometimes I thought about trying to find my way to Grandma Orene's house, but the thought of the man with the beard and what he might do to me would change my mind. But I missed them. I missed them both terribly. The only true good I had ever known in the world, existed in them.

Kenny even smiled and seemed happy for the first time in a long time that day. It was a good day, a day I never forgot.

***

Early that summer, my body started to change, started acting like it had a mind of its own. Things started shifting, growing in strange ways, and in no time, I began to look like a woman with budding breasts and a plumper behind. I wondered how that was possible when I was always so hungry, although I understood that these things happened to girls at a certain age. My cousin, Carrie, had told me all about it. She knew all of the facts because her mother had told her when she got her period the year before. But when I got mine for the first time that June, it still kind of scared me. Luckily, Carrie shared some of her pads with me and promised to always share them with me. It seemed that the older she got, the more she came to realize just how much alike we were despite the differences in our skin tones. It also helped that the more she began to look like a woman, herself, the meaner Uncle Teddy was toward her. We had begun to bond due to a mutual hatred for him. I saw that as a good thing. At least I had one semi-friend in the world now that Carrie was being kind to me since the only other friends I'd had were left behind in Milwaukee.

I felt awkward and clumsy in my new body, as if my skin had shifted around and I no longer fit in it. I felt self-conscious, too. Boys were always looking at me—boys that came to play with my cousin, Toby, boys in the yards we passed when we walked to the store and spent the change we'd find on the side of the road. Boys we met in the woods behind our house when we went out exploring. They all gave me the same odd look, like I was something new and shiny to them. Something special. No one had ever looked at me like that before and it bothered me. But what bothered me more than that was when Uncle Teddy started looking at me the same way.

14

"Sunshine"

Aunt Joyce came to see us!

She came to see us on the Fourth of July. We were outside playing—well, I was outside sitting under a shade tree with Kenny, watching my cousins play in some dirt—when a long, black car pulled up in the yard. We all stared at it, wondering whose it was. It was so glossy and clean and new-looking. It was the prettiest car I had ever seen. I was so amazed by it that I stood to my feet and kept my eyes glued to it as I waited for whoever was inside to step out. Uncle Teddy even came outside and stood on the porch with a curious look on his face.

When she stepped out, I wanted to cry. The last time I'd seen her, her face was all swollen and bruised and bloody. Before that, she'd been half out of her mind because of Uncle Larry's death. But that day in Uncle Teddy's yard, she looked so beautiful, just as beautiful as the first time I saw her. Her hair was in a huge afro and it shook and bounced with every step she took. She wore a short black leather skirt and a black tank top and sandals. She looked like a movie star even with the scar on her cheek—the remnants of the beating the bearded man had given her.

I watched as she walked toward the porch. I wanted to run to her, but I wasn't sure how Uncle Teddy would react or if he'd even allow her on his property. After all, he hated black people and I was sure he hadn't forgotten how crazy Aunt Joyce had talked to him in the past.

She nodded at him. "You remember me?" she asked. Her voice was cold; there was nothing friendly about it.

"You Kenny's sister," Uncle Teddy said.

"Mm-hmm. I'm here to see his kids. Patty said they're staying here."

There was a moment of silence that seemed to stretch on for days, and then he said, "They playing out here somewhere." He turned and went back into the house, slamming the door behind him.

She nodded again and before she could take a step, I ran straight to her, clasping my arms around her waist. Tears crowded my eyes as I breathed in her fresh scent. I was so glad to see her, to see anyone who had ever loved me. As she wrapped her arms around my body and squeezed, I shut my eyes tightly and wished time would stop for a moment. It had been so long since I'd felt someone hold me. It had been forever since I'd felt love from anyone. I didn't want the moment to end.

When I finally let her go, she stepped toward Kenny and pulled him into a hug, too. And then she just stared at both of us with tears in her eyes. She rubbed her hands over our heads and said, "Wait here. I'll be right back." Then she stepped onto the porch and knocked on the door. When Uncle Teddy opened the door and stuck his head outside, she said, "I'm gonna take them for a ride, get 'em some candy."

Uncle Teddy nodded, ducked back inside the house.

Kenny and I climbed into the car, into the front seat, our sweaty thighs sticking to the white and black leather. The car smelled so good and it was just as spotless on the inside as outside. Aunt Joyce started the car and turned on the radio. I smiled at the sound of the music as it flowed through the speakers. I tapped my feet and watched the world roll by as the wind blew in through the open windows and soothed my hot skin.

"What you know about James Brown, Chrissy? I see you over there tapping your feet," she said.

I smiled at her and shrugged. "I don't know."

She returned my smile. "You sure are a pretty girl. Both of y'all are pretty. Even you, Kenny," she said and tousled his hair. Kenny blushed. "You still like books, Chrissy? You read now?"

I nodded. "I read all the time. I love it!"

"This your car?" Kenny asked.

My head snapped in his direction. Those were the most words he'd spoken in months.

"No, it's my husband's car."

"Husband?" Kenny and I said in unison.

"Mm-hmm," she said.

I wondered if she'd married that white-looking man she was so crazy about. So I asked, "That light-skinned man your husband?"

She shook her head. "No, honey, I grew up and left that fool alone, stopped trading myself off for books and perfume. My husband's name is Yusef Porter. He's tall and dark-skinned and good-looking, a *real* man. We got married a couple of months ago."

"You love him?" I asked, remembering what she'd told me about love.

She shot me a grin. "Sometimes I do. It's okay to love sometimes, Chrissy."

I made note of that.

"How Grandma Orene doing?" I asked.

Aunt Joyce sighed. "Not too well. She's been kind of sick. She lives up north with her sister now. Better doctors up there. She misses y'all, though."

"We miss her, too," I said, speaking for both me and Kenny. Kenny nodded in agreement.

"How long y'all been living with your uncle?"

"Too long," I blurted.

As she pulled in front of the store and turned the car off, she said, "I bet." She shook her head and sighed as she pulled the key from the ignition. "Come on, y'all, let's get you some goodies. Anything you want."

Kenny and I almost broke our legs jumping out of that car and running into the store. She'd said we could get anything we wanted, and we took her at her word. We got some potato chips, some candy bars, and some soda. Then she took us for a long ride in her car and let us eat our stuff. "I can't let you take that stuff back with you. Those poor white trash cousins of yours will probably take it from you."

I couldn't argue with that because she was probably right.

She finally took us home right before dark and I wanted to cry. I didn't want her to leave and I didn't want to go back in that musty, dingy house.

"When was the last time you saw your mother?" she asked.

I shrugged. Kenny turned his head.

"When I talked to her, she said you guys were doing good. Talked like she sees you all the time."

No answer from me or Kenny.

"Y'all so skinny and… and…"

Dirty, I thought. That was the word she was looking for—dirty.

We all fell silent as we sat in Uncle Teddy's front yard. Kenny was staring at the house probably thinking the same thing I was, that he would've rather gone any other place in the world than back in that house. There was a light on in the living room, so I guessed they had finished dinner and were watching TV or something, which meant me and Kenny would have to sit in some corner on the floor until they all went to bed, making sure to keep our eyes off of Uncle Teddy or we'd end up on our hands and knees.

"They treating y'all okay?"

Before I could answer, Kenny shook his head. "No. We don't like it here."

"And they don't like us being here," I added.

"I figured. That man looks like a racist, damn white devil. I can see it in his eyes. Saw it that time he came over to Mama's house pretending to check on y'all, trying to be all nice, giving me that money, but I saw that hate behind his eyes. Wouldn't be surprised if he was one of the ones that helped kill Larry."

I gasped. "You really think so?" Now I really didn't want to go back in that house.

She closed her eyes and shook her head. "I shouldn't have said that. I was just talking. Don't pay what I say no mind, y'all."

We all fell silent again, then she said, "Y'all wanna go to church with me on Sunday? We can have dinner afterwards."

"Yes!" me and Kenny nearly screamed.

We climbed out of the car and Aunt Joyce walked us to the door and told Uncle Teddy she was picking us up for church on Sunday. He just nodded at her and told us to get on in the house.

***

I was glad to get to go to church with Aunt Joyce, but I was worried about what we were going to wear. I worried about that every minute up until we heard the knock at the front door that Sunday morning. I had chosen the best-looking hand-me-down dress I owned and Kenny had put on a pair of shorts and a black shirt, figuring it would look less dirty than a white shirt. We were sitting in the corner on the living room floor finishing up our breakfast when she came. Fortunately, Uncle Teddy was still asleep. He always slept late on Sundays since no one ever went to church in that house, so Sunday mornings were usually peaceful, or as peaceful as things could get there.

Aunt Tabitha answered the door and yelled, "Chrissy and Kenny!" without even really acknowledging Aunt Joyce. It amazed me that standing there in the doorway of a shack of a house with raggedy furniture and dingy clothes, she still thought she was better than Aunt Joyce who was dressed like a movie star in a turquoise flair skirt and matching jacket. She wore a soft yellow blouse underneath and her afro was shining like new money.

Kenny and I hopped to our feet and nearly leapt through the front door and into her car. Once we were inside, both of our skinny behinds resting on the passenger seat, Aunt Joyce reached into the backseat and pulled out a paper sack. She placed it on my lap and smiled at me. "For you two," she said as she backed out of the driveway.

I peered inside the sack and gasped as I began to remove its contents. There was a pretty pink shirt and black skirt for me and a blue and white striped shirt and dark blue shorts for Kenny. We were both so excited and happy, we were speechless. I reached over and wrapped my arms around her neck. She laughed and said, "You choking me, girl! I can't drive like this!"

"I'm sorry, Aunt Joyce, I just… thank you!"

"You're welcome, pretty girl," she said, rubbing her hand across my cheek while keeping the other one on the steering wheel. "We'll stop by the house so you two can get changed. I got some rubber bands so we can fix your hair while we're there, Chrissy."

I nodded and looked over at Kenny whose eyes were bright. He smiled at me and I smiled right back at him, knowing he was just as happy as I was to get to be the first person to wear those clothes.

15

"Black Man"

I almost cried when Aunt Joyce pulled into Grandma Orene's front yard. She said that was where she and her husband were living. It felt good to be back there. Good… and scary. What about the man? How could Aunt Joyce even stand to be there?

When she stopped the engine and opened her door, I just sat there—frozen. When Kenny opened the passenger door and waited for me, I still sat there. The air around me suddenly felt cold, as if the summer heat had quickly evaporated. I no longer wanted to go to church. As a matter of fact, I almost wanted to go back to Uncle Teddy's house… *almost*.

"Chrissy?" she said, leaning over and peering into the car at me.

I looked up at her but couldn't reply. My throat was dry and my eyes were wet.

She stood there and looked at me for a minute or two and then she said, "Kenny, take the sack and go on inside."

She slid back into the driver's seat as I watched Kenny trot to the house. "He's dead," she said.

I frowned as I turned to face her. Who was dead?

As if reading my thoughts, she said, "The man who hurt me and threatened to hurt you? He's dead."

I turned back to the house. "How you know that?"

She reached over and rested her hand on my bony thigh. I looked up at her as a tear began to trickle down my cheek. "Because I know who killed him. I... saw it happen," she said softly.

My eyes widened. "You did?"

She nodded and turned to the house in silence. I followed her gaze to see a man standing on the porch with a concerned look on his face. He was tall and dark with broad shoulders and he was very handsome with wide eyes and full lips. He looked how I imagined a king would look standing in front of his palace, ready to defend his country at all costs—powerful. "Yusef saved my life that night. That's when I knew I had to marry him. That's when I fell in love with him." She turned to face me. "That's when I found out it's okay to love sometimes."

"He killed the man?"

She nodded. "Promise not to tell anyone?"

"I promise. Will you tell me how it happened?"

She gave me a small smile. "After church."

***

That night, after church and the singing and the moaning from the old ladies and the foot stomping of the deacons. After the greens and cornbread and neck bones that Aunt Joyce cooked that almost but didn't quite taste like Grandma Orene's. After Yusef took Kenny for ice cream and Aunt Joyce and I sat on the front porch and talked. After me and Kenny took off our new clothes and left them at our grandmother's house and wore our old hand-me-downs back home. After Uncle Teddy stopped yelling and screaming at everyone in the house. After Aunt Tabitha stopped crying because he slapped her. After the stinging of where his belt hit my back because I was smiling when I walked back into his house stopped hurting so bad. After Kenny fell asleep. After all in the house was quiet, I thought about what Aunt Joyce had told me. About how the man with the beard had seen her when she and Yusef came back from where they had been living in Little Rock to help Grandma Orene move up north. How he had come knocking at the door late one night and how she had panicked and gone number one on herself because she was so scared. She said Yusef had answered the door and said, "We don't have no business with you and you don't have no business with us. Now, it'd be best for you to leave."

"You a real uppity nigger, huh? Think you can talk to a white man like that, do you? I've lynched better men than you!" the man had said.

Aunt Joyce said Yusef never flinched. He just stood in the doorway, his shoulders squared. She said she'd never seen a black man be so brave in all her life. "Ain't gon' be no lynching here tonight, sir."

She said the man laughed real loud like he thought Yusef was joking. She said Yusef never cracked a smile.

"Now look here, nigger. That gal in there? I'm gonna have some time with her, you hear? And when I'm done, you can do what you want with her."

"No, sir. You ain't gon' touch her."

Aunt Joyce said the man grinned, spit tobacco onto Yusef's bare foot, and said, "I done already touched her. She put up a good fight, too. But I loved that about her. Hope she still got some fight in her for me tonight."

She said the next thing she knew, Yusef had punched the man. She said the man flew off the porch into the front yard. She said she screamed and so did Grandma Orene, who could hear the commotion from her room. She said Yusef hit the man so many times she lost count. By the time she touched his shoulder and begged him to stop, the man was dead.

"I'm so glad that man came over here by himself that night, but I guess he didn't want his clan friends to know he liked black women. I heard I wasn't the first black woman he raped and I wouldn't have been the last one if Yusef hadn't done what he did. Anyway, since he was alone, there wasn't no witnesses and me and Mama sure ain't gon' never say nothing. I believe that man killed Larry, too. I really do. Anyhow, Yusef dragged him out of the yard and put him in the bed of his own truck, then he drove all the way to the river and rolled that truck into the water. White folks still don't know what happened to him, but I heard his wife done moved away from here. Folks say she was glad he went missing. Seems he was a bastard to her, too."

I smiled in the darkness as I wondered if Yusef would kill Uncle Teddy for me if I asked him to.

16

"Getaway"

For three Sundays in a row Aunt Joyce picked us up and took us to church. And every time she picked us up, she'd have a new outfit waiting for us in the car. She always made us leave the clothes at her house because, as she said, "I don't trust those poor white folks. They'll probably take these clothes from y'all and give them to their kids." I thought she was probably right.

I wondered if she was rich or something now. How could she afford the clothes she wore, the clothes she bought for us, the new car? There was even new furniture in Grandma Orene's house. When I asked her about it, she chuckled and said, "No, I'm not rich but Yusef is. He come from money and his folks don't mind sharing it with him." She said she'd actually met him at Grandma Orene's church when she was still recovering from what the man with the beard did to her, said he had family in England, Arkansas, he was visiting at the time.

Yusef was always really nice to me and Kenny, always smiled at us, and despite being so big and tall, his voice was always gentle when he spoke to us. I liked him... a lot. I felt weird inside when he was around. He was my uncle, but he didn't feel like he was my uncle. I understood why Aunt Joyce loved him. Sometimes I thought I loved him, too. Or maybe it was just that next to Mr. Henry, he was the nicest man I'd ever known. My memory of my own father had all but faded by then, so I couldn't remember if he was nice to me or not. As a matter of fact, all I remembered was him arguing with my mother or making the squeaky mattress squeak even louder with her. That was it. Those things were on my mind that Sunday when I blurted, "My daddy is dead," to Aunt Joyce while we were sitting on the front porch together after dinner like we always did. I had no idea why I said it. I guess I'd held the secret in for so long, it couldn't help but burst out.

She frowned slightly as she looked me in the eye. "Why you say that, Chrissy?"

"I heard my mama telling her husband about it."

"Your mama said she never found him."

"My mama lies a lot."

Aunt Joyce nodded. "I think you're right about that." A sadness seemed to cover her entire body. "Did she say how he died?"

I nodded. "She said he owed some money and that got him killed."

She hung her head and sighed.

"She didn't want to upset Grandma Orene, so she didn't tell y'all."

"Well, I'm glad she didn't tell Mama. We had already figured it out, though. No way Kenny Ray would stay gone this long and not check on Mama. It's been years, like six or seven years. And he was crazy about you and your brother, too. Wouldn't have left y'all this long."

"He was? I mean, he was crazy about us?"

She cocked her head to the side. "You were so young when he left. You don't remember him, huh?"

"I remember a little."

"Well, he loved you and your brother very much. Does little Kenny know he died?"

I shook my head. "I didn't tell him."

She smiled. "You're a good big sister for protecting him from that, Chrissy."

***

When she dropped us off back at home, she walked us to the door and greeted Uncle Teddy who just grunted in response. Then she said, "I'm gonna talk to Patty about letting the kids stay with me and my husband for a while. I've already discussed it with him and everything. I'm sure you'll be glad for me to take them off your hands."

Uncle Teddy just stood there and stared at her.

"Well, have a good evening," she said as she turned to leave.

I was so surprised and excited that I stood in the middle of the living room and stared at Uncle Teddy's back. And when he turned to face me, I forgot to drop my eyes or bow. Kenny remembered, but for the first time in a long time, I didn't. I was too excited to remember, and evidently, I was smiling, too. At least that was what Uncle Teddy said when he hit me: "Wipe that smile off your face, you little mongrel!"

Then he hit me again and again. He hit me until he got tired, then he cussed at me for hurting his hand. I went to bed with a busted lip and a bruised cheek that night and my little brother holding me tight, telling me it was going to be okay like he was the oldest and not me. When I closed my swollen eyes, I thanked God for Aunt Joyce, for her saving us from that place and that man.

***

Early that next Wednesday morning, Aunt Tabitha woke me and Kenny up and told us to get dressed. I looked up at her and then sat up and looked around the room. The furniture was gone—all of it. The TV was even gone, and when I saw that, it felt like someone reached inside my chest, wrapped their hand around my heart, and squeezed. The furniture being gone was one thing, but the TV? Uncle Teddy loved that TV. As a matter of fact, I was sure that was the only thing in the world he cared about at all. At that point, I was almost certain Kenny and I weren't going anywhere with Aunt Joyce. They were leaving and they were taking us with them. They were taking us away just to be evil. Or maybe… just maybe, they were taking us to Aunt Joyce's. That was a hopeful thought, but one that didn't seem very realistic. I was young, but I had sense enough to know that Uncle Teddy enjoyed spending my mother's money. I was pretty sure he'd be willing to keep me and Kenny around just for the purpose of getting her money.

As Kenny sat up beside me with curiosity in his eyes, I looked toward the kitchen to see that the table and chairs were missing. I got to my feet in my t-shirt and underwear and peeped out the front door. Uncle Teddy's pick-up truck was loaded down with furniture, and there were other trucks in the yard, too—all loaded with furniture. Tears stung my eyes as I turned around and looked at Aunt Tabitha as she dropped a cardboard box on the floor and said, "Put y'all's stuff in here. We're leaving in thirty minutes."

"Does our mother know?" I asked with a shaky voice. I really didn't care if she knew or not. I just had to say something.

"Of course she does," she said as she turned and walked down the hall. I didn't see or hear my cousins or Uncle Teddy and that was a good thing. I didn't want to see or hear them at that moment.

I walked back over to where me and Kenny slept, grabbed the cover off of him, and began folding it up. He did the same with the quilt we slept on top of. "Where we going?" he asked barely above a whisper.

I shrugged. "Away from here, I guess," I said, trying to put up a brave front.

"What about Aunt Joyce?"

"I don't know. Maybe she'll find us."

Heavy footsteps entered the house. "Hurry up!" Uncle Teddy shouted.

Kenny and I quickly dressed and shoved our few clothes into the box. All of our clothes—his and mine—fit easily into it and we each only had two pairs of shoes—a winter pair and a summer pair. We wore our summer shoes and carried our winter shoes in our hands. Our empty stomachs grumbled as Uncle Teddy directed us to get in the truck with him. Carrie and Toby rode in another truck with their mother and a man I had seen a couple of times before and recognized as Aunt Tabitha's brother.

We were riding down the highway when curiosity finally got the best of Kenny and he asked, "Where we going?"

There was silence as I held my breath, waiting for Uncle Teddy to backhand Kenny or yell at him or stop the truck, pull him outside, and beat him with a belt, but he did none of that. He just kept his eyes ahead of him and said nothing. Kenny didn't say anything else, either. We both watched the scenery that passed by so fast you could barely tell a tree from a house. The ride wasn't that long, and I tried to commit the names of the towns we passed through to memory in case I ever got to call Aunt Joyce and tell her where we were. She had told me her phone number that first Sunday we went to church with her and I never forgot it. In my mind, I repeated the names of churches, highways, stores, anything. And then we made it to the biggest city I'd ever seen—Little Rock—and before I could stop myself, I said, "We're moving to Little Rock?" Then I braced myself for what I was once again sure was to come.

He merely glanced at me and nodded.

Suddenly the knots in my hollow stomach were replaced with the fluttering butterflies of excitement. The buildings were so tall and there were so many cars! Suddenly, the sorrow of not being able to live with Aunt Joyce fled my mind and in its place was something my young heart hadn't felt in a long time—the possibility of hope. I felt like I was on an adventure of some sort. Kind of like the ones I'd read about in my books. Then I remembered I'd forgotten to bring my books with me. In our hurry to leave, I hadn't even thought about them. Maybe I could find a way to get some more. Surely, I could. This was Little Rock, the big city. I was certain that anything was possible there.

17

"The Changing Times"

Things were different in Little Rock, better. In Little Rock, we lived in a much nicer house and Kenny and I even got to share a bedroom and we got a mattress! Sure, it was a handed-down one our cousins used to sleep on, and if you moved around too much on it, you would stir up the scent of urine that undoubtedly belonged to Toby who, at twelve years old, still wet the bed (but with a father like his, who could blame him?). And it was only given to us because our cousins were the recipients of a brand spanking new set of bunk beds, but still, it was a mattress and it was much more comfortable to sleep on than the floor. There was a washer and dryer in the house so we were able to keep our hand-me-downs clean without having to wash them by hand. That had been so hard to do that Kenny had given up washing his clothes ages ago and though I tried to keep mine clean, they were still dingy.

There were two bathrooms and the water was always hot so I got to take baths a couple of days a week. Me and Kenny still had to eat on the floor and we still got the least amount of food, but Uncle Teddy was a little nicer to us and he relaxed his rules a bit. We (and by we, I mean everyone who lived in that house with him) still weren't allowed to look him in the eye, but we were no longer required to bow in his presence.

The neighborhood was diverse in comparison to where we lived before, and most of the people were nice to us. When school started, we attended the same one as Carrie and Toby. And I loved school! What I loved most was the library. I checked out a different book every week! I read a ton of books that first year and still wanted to read more. I did well in school, made A's. But I'd always loved learning about things, especially art and history.

We didn't hear from Aunt Joyce after we moved to Little Rock, because I was sure she had no idea where we moved to. I would often imagine her showing up at the house the Sunday after we moved away and finding that old shack empty. I would wonder what she felt when she realized we were gone. Did she ask around or look for us? Did Yusef help? If she called my mother and asked where we were, did my mother tell her the truth or did she lie? I hadn't been able to call her, because we didn't have a phone in Little Rock and I never had money for a pay phone.

And our mother? I wasn't even sure how I felt about her anymore. I mean, I knew I hated her, but it wasn't a fierce hate like before. It was more of a dismissive, out of sight, out of mind numbness-type hate. I hated her for leaving us behind, but I didn't want to be with her, either. After her only visit to check on us, she hadn't returned. It had been well over a year and we hadn't had any contact at all with her. There were times when I wondered if she was even still alive, but then I realized her money was probably how Uncle Teddy managed to move us into such a nice house.

I still hated him, but I liked living in Little Rock. I almost liked my life, too. Kenny seemed happier, and at that point, we were both sure things could only get better for us.

18

"Where Have All the Flowers Gone"

1973

"Chrissy, get up."

The harsh whisper came in the middle of the night and I was so deeply asleep, I could've sworn I dreamed it. I stirred a bit and then rolled over without opening my eyes.

Someone softly shook my shoulder and this time, I realized what was happening was really happening. I sat up straight and Kenny murmured something before continuing to sleep. I glanced around the dark room and when my eyes adjusted, I saw him. Uncle Teddy was crouched beside our mattress, staring at me. I automatically dropped my eyes and whispered, "Uncle Teddy?"

"Come with me," he said.

I groggily stood from the mattress. I had no idea where we were going, but I knew better than to disobey him. I followed him down the hall, through the living room, through the kitchen, and out into the backyard in my bare feet, wearing nothing but a thin t-shirt and panties. My eyes were glued to the back of his dingy white t-shirt as he stopped at the little shed in the backyard. It had come with the house and he'd claimed it as his work shed. No one was allowed in it but him. I stood in the frigid night air and watched as he unlocked the shed. He opened the door and beckoned for me to go inside. Unsure of what was going on, I did the only thing I knew to do: I did what he said.

Once we were inside, he reached up and pulled a chain; a naked light bulb illuminated our surroundings. The space smelled strongly of gasoline due to a half-filled metal gas can sitting in a corner. As he closed and padlocked the door, I glanced around. There was a workbench with a hammer and nails strewn on it. There was a lawn mower, a wheel barrow, and two chairs that had been a part of the dinette set in the old house. The sofa from the old house was also in there. Uncle Teddy plopped down on it and looked at me. It felt strange to be stared at like that so I dropped my eyes and twisted my hands in front of me.

"You sure are getting pretty," he finally said.

When I looked up, he was smiling at me. That felt even stranger, so I dropped my eyes again.

"You're supposed to say, 'thank you'."

"Uh… thank you," I muttered.

"Come sit with me, Chrissy."

With my eyes still downcast, I closed the distance between us and sat at the far end of the sofa from him. He scooted closer to me and rested his hand on my thigh. I flinched and a shudder raced through my body.

"It's okay," he said softly.

But in my heart, I knew it wasn't okay.

"You cold?"

Rather than voice a lie, I merely shook my head.

He leaned in so close to me that I could feel his hot breath on my cheek. I could smell it, too. It smelled like tobacco. "You smell real sweet, Chrissy."

I closed my eyes and remembering my manners, said, "Thank you." I shivered from more than the cold air that infused the small space.

I felt him kiss my cheek and my entire body locked up. I wanted to run, but I was afraid to. I was just afraid, *period*. But I was also oddly happy because he was being nice to me, the nicest he'd ever been.

I felt the rough skin of his hand on my cheek, then another kiss, then... nothing. I could feel his body heat, so I knew he was still sitting next to me, but he wasn't moving or saying anything. After several minutes of nothing surrounding us but silence, I opened one eye to see him staring at me, smiling at me. I quickly closed it again. Several minutes later, he said, "Come on, let's go back in the house."

I followed him inside and fell back onto the mattress with Kenny.

"Where you been?" Kenny asked. I could tell he was more asleep than awake.

"Nowhere," I replied.

***

Uncle Teddy roused me out of bed and took me to his shed every night for the next two weeks. We would sit on the couch together, or sometimes I would sit on the couch and he would sit in one of the old kitchen chairs right in front of me and just stare at me. Sometimes he would kiss my cheek or hold my hand, tell me I was pretty and that I smelled good. Other times, he'd show me his magazines that he kept hidden in the shed, the ones with the naked women. I hated looking at those and didn't know why he showed them to me.

Being with him in that shed never felt exactly right, but then again, it never felt exactly wrong, either. I was thirteen and I hadn't been held or kissed even on the forehead by anyone in a long time. When we would see Aunt Joyce, she might pat our hand or head or cheek, but she only occasionally hugged us and she never kissed us. I hadn't felt my mother's or father's arms around me in what felt like forever and up until that point, all my uncle had given me was lashes from a belt and slaps to my face. There was Kenny, but he was getting older and no longer liked to cuddle with me. I was craving some affection from someone, *anyone*, and in my mind, a kiss on the cheek here or there from Uncle Teddy was better than nothing.

I knew he wanted to keep our time together a secret without him even telling me. I figured he didn't want his own kids to get jealous since I'd never seen him be very loving to them or to Aunt Tabitha, for that matter.

One night, while I was sitting there next to him with my eyes closed, I felt the kiss on my lips instead of my cheek. My eyes flew open. Now, *this* felt wrong, *very* wrong. I shot to my feet, breaking our contact. He looked up at me and said, "It's okay," as he reached for my hand. "It's okay, Chrissy."

My mind screamed, "No, it's not! It's not okay!" But the words crashed behind my teeth, never reaching my lips. All I managed to do was gulp frosty air, shake my head, and continue to back away from him. He stood next to me, several inches taller than me. He was skinny, but he was a man and he was strong and I knew it, but still, once I saw the look in his muddy green eyes, I did what came natural to me. I ran toward the shed door. I wanted to run as fast as I could and get away from that place and him forever. But he easily caught up with me in the small space, grabbed me, and shoved me to the floor. And right then, I realized what it had all been about—the late night visits to the shed, the hand-holding, the kisses, the compliments, the smiles. It had all been leading up to this moment, to this glimmer in time.

It had all been leading up to him raping me.

19

"Deep In It"

I lay there on the cold, dirty concrete floor of the shed with a throbbing headache, my ripped panties lying beside me. My entire body was sore, my stomach churned. My eyes were swollen from unrelenting tears. My heart was broken. Uncle Teddy lay next to me, breathing loudly and rapidly, the back of his hand resting on his forehead. I had fought him with everything in me. I had kicked and screamed so loudly that he'd finally clamped a sour-smelling hand over my mouth to quiet me. He had hit me so many times I was sure my face was a bruised mess. And in the end, he had won the battle. He had taken from me what was supposed to be mine and mine alone to give. I gagged at the thought of what had just happened. I held my hand over my mouth before flipping over and vomiting on the floor. Uncle Teddy reached up on the sofa, grabbed a towel, and handed it to me. "You sick? Something you ate? Probably so with Tabitha's cooking. I don't know what the hell that was we ate tonight."

I didn't answer, just wiped the remnants of my dinner from the floor and tried not to vomit again, wished I could disappear.

"I was your mama's first love and she was mine. You know that?" he said matter-of-factly as he stared at me.

I shook my head, no, in response, kept wiping the floor.

"Shoot, I almost coulda been your daddy." He chuckled. He was obviously amusing himself. "We started messing around when I was about your age; she was about ten. Back then, our ma and pa would leave to go on trips with the church and such, and I'd have to stay behind and watch Patty. We used to mess around all the time. At first we was just kids playing around and stuff, and then we'd started to really liking it. Shoot, after a while, Patty *loved* it. She loved me, too."

Somehow I doubted he knew how she truly felt about him and I doubted she loved doing *anything* with him, least of all *that*.

"You know, that kinda lovin' runs in the family. My ma and pa is second cousins. Anyway, Patty went off to college and when she came back, she was acting all different. Didn't want to mess around anymore 'cause I'd married Tabitha. I told her that didn't matter none. Shoot, I didn't care nothing about Tabitha, still don't. I just needed someone to cook and clean and have my kids. Wasn't like I could marry Patty or nothing like that. But still, she told me no, that we couldn't do it no more. So I went on about my business. Didn't pay her no more mind. Then she started up with your daddy." He paused and shook his head. "I just didn't understand why she'd rather give herself to a damn coon than to be with me!"

He sat up and stared into space for a minute. I reached up and rubbed my sore jaw, tried to clear the bile from my throat.

"I was done with her. Didn't talk to her for a long time. She had you and your brother and everything and I just acted like she was dead. I was mad as a hornet at her. Ma and Pa were, too." He rubbed his forehead and smiled. "Then she came to visit Ma and Pa one day and I happened to be over there at the same time. Them old feelings came back to me, you know? And I could see she felt the same way.

"I walked her home that day. You kids was outside playing and your daddy wasn't home, so we went inside the house and messed around some. At first she acted like she didn't wanna do it, but she eventually gave in."

He smiled at me, but it wasn't the warm, inviting smile he'd given me so many nights before. It was more of a sneer. "Your daddy caught us. He was so mad, he got his stuff and left. Never did come back. Patty told folks he went up north to look for work. Truth is, he went up there because of what he saw us doing." He reached over and rested his hand on my cheek. "I loved your mama, Chrissy. I really did, but the moment I saw you, way back when you and your brother were living with Kenny's folks, I knew I'd love you more than I ever loved her. And I do. I really do. You love me, too?"

I wanted to say no. I wanted to jump up and grab that hammer and bash his brains in. Instead, I just nodded, yes.

***

I lied about my bruises and my swollen jaw, said I stumbled and fell on the way to the bathroom that night. I don't think anyone really believed me, but they didn't say they didn't believe me, either. From that night on, he took me to the shed nearly every night. He didn't kiss me or hold my hand anymore. Instead, he just took my body from me over and over again. At first, I would always fight him—sometimes a lot and other times, I'd be so tired and sore I could only fight a little; either way, he had to know I didn't want to do it. Then, I came to realize he liked that part of it, me fighting him. So I just stopped fighting and let it happen as I knew it would anyway.

The day after that first time, there was a gift waiting for me after school—a real pretty dress. And there were more gifts to come— books, little bottles of perfume, dolls. He didn't even bother to cover up what he was doing by getting his kids gifts. He didn't seem to care that his favoritism was obvious. Aunt Tabitha knew something was going on. I could see it in how she looked at me the night he announced I could sit at the dinner table and eat with them. I refused to leave Kenny on the floor, so he said he could come to the table, too. Something shifted in me after that. I came to realize that I had a certain power over him. That same night, when he took me to the shed, I asked him if he would buy Kenny this comic book he'd been wanting. He said he'd think about it and the next day after school, lo and behold, there was the comic book sitting on our mattress right next to a shiny new copy of *Alice in Wonderland* for me. I asked if me and Kenny could have a new mattress; he got us a new set of bunk beds. When we were alone, he'd tell me how much he loved me and needed me. And after a while, I started to believe him.

One day, Uncle Teddy took me out of school early and brought me home with him. By that time Aunt Tabitha had gotten a job as a waitress at a restaurant so the house was empty. That day we did it in his bed and the bed felt good, much better than the shed floor. I still didn't like doing it with him, but I liked lying in that bed and I looked forward to whatever gift he would give me next. But it was really weird to do it in the daytime. Somehow it felt even more wrong, like God could see us better or something.

When we were finished, he did like he always did. He lay next to me staring at the ceiling and talking, telling me intimate things. "I couldn't wait till tonight, Chrissy. Do you know how much I love you?"

He shifted his eyes to me. As always, I shook my head.

"I love you more than anything, Chrissy. *Anything*. I wanna marry you one day if the law will allow it. They should, you know? People in the Bible used to do it. Ain't nothing wrong with what we feel for each other. I'm so glad we moved from down home. I really feel like we can be together now…" He went on and on and on. He was talking to me, but it always felt like he was trying to convince himself with his own words.

We talked and messed around until right before he knew Kenny and Carrie and Toby would be home, then we left and he bought me a hamburger and a shake. When we made it back, Kenny asked, "Why you leave school early? Somebody said Uncle Teddy came and got you."

"I was sick," I said, repeating the lie Uncle Teddy had instructed me to tell.

"You don't look sick now."

"I feel better."

He didn't believe me but before he could say anything else, we were both startled by Aunt Tabitha's shrieking voice. "You been cheating on me in my own bed, Teddy?! You didn't even try to hide it! You didn't even make the bed back up!"

"Who the hell are you yelling at?! I told you I got to feeling bad at work and came home and took a nap!" Uncle Teddy yelled back.

"You're lying! I *know* you're lying!"

Smack!

"Did you lose your mind? Those burgers and fries you peddling give you amnesia? Don't you ever, *ever* raise your voice at me again!"

"You think I don't know what you been doing with that little girl? I know... *I know*," she said through a whimper.

"What little girl are you talking about?"

Silence.

I could only imagine the look on his face at that moment. She was probably too scared to say another word.

When I looked at Kenny again, he was staring at me as if he expected me to say something. I said nothing. I just left our room and headed to the living room to watch TV. I had only been sitting on the sofa a couple of minutes before Uncle Teddy came and sat next to me.

***

I hadn't expected Uncle Teddy to take me to the shed that night, but he did. Early the next morning, when I climbed back onto the bottom bunk, I was surprised when Kenny's whisper filled the room. "What y'all be doing out there in that shed?" he asked.

I was so stunned by his question, I said the first thing that came to my mind in response, "Nothing."

"Whatever you do out there, is that why he keeps getting us stuff?"

I hesitated and then said, "Yeah."

"You like doing it?"

"No—I don't know."

"It's wrong, you know."

"Yeah, I know."

"You like him now?"

"Sometimes I think I do."

"He likes you now."

"I know."

"I still hate him."

"I know."

When we woke up the next morning, Aunt Tabitha was gone and so were my cousins.

That next night, Uncle Teddy moved me into his bedroom.

I was thirteen years old.

20

"Save the Children"

"Oh, my goodness! Look how you've grown! I missed you two so much!"

I stood frozen as the chirpy voice filled my ears, inadvertently blocking Kenny from entering the house and leaving him standing in the rain that was pouring down. "What's going on?" he asked as he tried to shove past me. He finally succeeded at entering the house and upon seeing our mother, dropped his books on the floor and raced into her arms. Still, I just stood there. I could see Uncle Teddy standing in the corner of the living room and I could feel his eyes on me. The only thought in my head was that now that she was here, she was going to mess up the good thing I had going with Uncle Teddy. I probably wouldn't get another gift until after she left.

"Chrissy? You gonna come give me a hug?"

I looked at her all decked out in an orange jumpsuit and I felt my lunch begin to inch up my throat. I dropped my own books and raced to the bathroom where I heaved until there was nothing left to heave but bile.

"Chrissy… are you all right, sweetie?" came her voice through the closed bathroom door.

I didn't answer her. I washed my face with cold water and stared at myself in the mirror for a moment before stepping out of the bathroom and shoving past her.

"Chrissy?" she said as I made my way to the room I had shared with Uncle Teddy for the past several months and shut the door.

"Chrissy? Can I talk to you, sweetie?" she asked through the door.

I sat on the side of the bed and tried not to cry. My emotions were in a tumble. I was scared for her to know what had been going on with Uncle Teddy and scared for her not to know. I was glad and mad about seeing her at the same time. I just didn't know how to feel.

The bedroom door creaked open and in walked Uncle Teddy. Mama was standing in the doorway behind him. He shut the door in her face and sat down on the bed next to me. "You okay?" he asked.

I nodded.

He nodded, too. "You should probably sleep in your old bed while she's here."

I nodded again and then stood to leave. He grasped my arm to stop me. "I love you, Chrissy," he whispered.

"I love you, too," I whispered back.

That night we all sat around the table and ate Kentucky Fried Chicken for dinner. We'd been eating out every night since Aunt

Tabitha left. Me and Kenny didn't mind that at all since Aunt Tabitha was a bad cook anyway.

"So, where are Tabitha and the kids?" Mama asked in the middle of dinner.

"I don't know," Uncle Teddy said with a shrug.

"What do you mean, *you don't know?* I just asked you about your wife and kids, not some strangers."

"I mean, *I don't know*, Patty," he said with a tinge of irritation in his voice.

"Well, what happened with you two?"

"She forgot her place and I told her to take her kids and get out of my house."

"They're your kids, too, Teddy."

"Yeah, that's what she says."

There were a few moments of silence and then my mother said, "Well, I'm glad you and Chrissy and Kenny are getting along so well now."

Kenny dropped his fork. I dropped my eyes.

Uncle Teddy laid his fork on his plate and leaned back in his chair. "What are you doing here out of the blue, Patty? You ain't been here to check on these kids in almost two years. What brings you here today?"

She straightened her posture and wiped her mouth with a paper napkin. "Well, when I spoke to Tabitha—"

"When you spoke to who?" Uncle Teddy interrupted.

"Tabitha. She called me a week ago and said I should really come and check on my kids, that they needed me. Well, when I talk to her again, I'll just have to tell her she's wrong. As far as I can see, everything is fine."

Kenny cleared his throat and glared at me. I shook my head.

"Everything is okay, isn't it, kids?" my mother said.

"No," Kenny said.

My heart began to gallop.

"What's wrong, Kenny?" Mama asked with concern in her eyes. Made me want to throw up again.

"Something's wrong with Chrissy," Kenny said.

Mama locked her gaze on me. "What's wrong, Chrissy? You sick?"

I looked up at Uncle Teddy, who was staring at me, and said, "Ain't nothing wrong with me."

Kenny hopped up from the table and shouted, "She's lying! Ask her where she sleeps at night!"

"I sleep in our room," I said. I knew what Kenny was trying to do and I knew he was right to do it, but I hated her and Uncle Teddy had come to mean something good to me.

Kenny stormed from the table without another word.

"Kenny!" she called after him.

"Let him go," Uncle Teddy said. "Just being a kid."

Mama looked from Uncle Teddy to me and then she just nodded.

We finished dinner in silence.

✳✳✳

"Chrissy... Chrissy, come with me."

The familiar whisper didn't wake me this time because I wasn't even asleep, having found it hard to drift off in a bed I was no longer used to sleeping in. I automatically climbed out of bed and quietly followed him to his room—*our* room. I slid into the familiarity of his sheets and his arms with ease. This had become normal to me. I closed my eyes and allowed it to happen as if it was right, because I had reached a point where right and wrong were blurring together and I could no longer keep track of the differences between the two. It was wrong for Uncle Teddy to do this to me, but it was right to feel love from someone. It was wrong to like being with him, but it was right to want to be with somebody, wasn't it?

With my eyes closed, sometimes I would choose to go other places when we did it. I would go to the places in the books I'd read—like the pyramids of Giza that I'd read about in a book about Egypt that Uncle Teddy had bought me. Or Oz, or somewhere else, anywhere else. Other times, I'd watch our shadows on the wall and pretend we were dancing to the strange music the squeaky springs of the mattress made. But this time, I chose to stay in the present and to stay aware of my surroundings. That was why I was the first to notice the bedroom door as it creaked open in the darkness. I was the first to see my mother's eyes widen in shock. I was the first to see Kenny standing in the doorway behind her.

"Uncle Teddy," I whispered.

He stopped and looked up at me, probably having sensed something in my voice, but before he could move a muscle, my mother had jumped on his back and was swinging her fists like a wild woman.

"Get off of her! Get off of her!" she screamed.

A couple of her wild blows hit me by accident. There was so much screaming and yelling you would've thought there was a crowd of people in that bedroom. I felt relieved in a way. Glad that the secret was out. Happy to be rescued. Sad to be rescued, too.

"You bastard! How long have you been raping my baby?! How long?!"

By now, Uncle Teddy was out of the bed and on his feet, naked as a jaybird and deflecting the blows from my mother. Kenny was still standing in the doorway. I pulled the sheet over my body, unsure of what I was supposed to do.

"She's just a baby! Just like *I* was a baby, you sick son-of-a—"

"She ain't no baby, Patty!" Uncle Teddy shouted. "Not no more! I done turned her into a woman!"

She lit into him again, punching and kicking wildly. He grabbed her arms and by the way she yelped, he must've squeezed them. "You need to calm down! I don't know why you are in here acting like this! You knew what I was when you left her with me! You knew damn well she was too pretty for me not to want her. You *knew*, Patty! Hell, I thought maybe this is what you wanted, for me and her to be together."

"What I wanted?! Are you insane?! She's your niece! I wanted and trusted you to take care of her, *not* violate her!"

"So what she's my niece?! You were my sister, weren't you? What damn difference does it make? And I didn't violate her. I love her. I wanna marry her."

"You love her?! You hate black people so much, I never thought you'd want to do this to her!"

He gazed over at me while touching himself. "She's only half black, and she's different. She's real special to me. Especially since she's filled out and everything. I bet if we had babies, they'd be white." He turned to Mama. "What do you think, Patty? What do you think our babies would look like?" He walked over to me and kissed me and rested his hand on my belly. "You think she's carrying one of my babies right now? I hope so."

Mama smacked him in the back of the head.

He pushed her to the floor.

As she struggled back to her feet she said, "Teddy, you are a sick—"

"Are you really gonna stand here and act like you care about what I do to her? You don't give a damn about either of these kids and you know it! I love that girl more than you ever have or ever will!"

"I love my kids, Teddy. They mean the world to me. The world…" she said with an uneven voice. Kenny moved toward her and Uncle Teddy screamed, "Get out of here, Kenny!"

Kenny quickly backed out of the room.

"Patty, you need to leave. Go on back up north. Everything's fine here. We don't need you."

Mama was shaking like a leaf. "I'll leave, but I'm taking my kids with me."

"No, you ain't."

"Yes, I am!"

"You can take Kenny, but not Chrissy. If you wanted her, you should have taken her back before me and her got started. You can't have her now. You can't take her from me!"

She turned to me. "Chrissy, get up and put some clothes on. You, too, Kenny. We're leaving right now!"

I didn't move a muscle.

"Christina Dandridge! Get up, *now!*"

"I don't wanna go," I said. For a second, I didn't even know if I'd really said it. For much longer than a second, I didn't know *why* I'd said it.

Uncle Teddy stepped between me and Mama. "I told you she ain't going nowhere. She likes being with me. Now, take your son and get the hell out of here." He backed up toward the doorway. "Chrissy stays with me."

There was a loud thud and a cracking sound and almost instantly, Uncle Teddy slumped to the floor. Behind him stood my skinny little brother, who was now taller than me, with a hammer in his hand. Forgetting my nakedness, I sprung from the bed and fell to the floor next to my uncle, cradling his bloody head in my lap.

"What did you do, Kenny? What did you do?!" I yelled through tears.

21

"Devotion"

He was dead.

Kenny killed him.

And as I sat there on the floor and watched the life leave his eyes, my mother paced back and forth, her hand to her mouth as she said, "Oh, no," over and over again. Kenny just stood there and stared at the floor in shock. My tears would not stop.

My heart was breaking. Uncle Teddy had loved me. I knew that to be true because he'd told me over and over again. No one else had told me as many times as he did. *No one.* And now he was gone. He'd never be able to tell me again.

"I need to think of something. Kenny, give me that hammer."

Kenny didn't move a muscle.

Mama said something else but by then, I had tuned her out. All I could hear were my own sniffles and my own ragged breathing. What was I supposed to do now?

She must've called the police and an ambulance because before I knew what was happening, the house was filled with people in uniforms—blue ones, black ones, white ones. Someone had draped a sheet around me, covering my exposed, still-developing body. Suddenly, I looked down and my uncle was gone. I blinked, and I was in a hospital room wearing a paper gown. I blinked again, and there was a policeman in the room with me, gently asking me questions. "Your mother says he raped you. That's why your brother hit him. Is that true?"

"Yes," I said, my eyes focused on a speck on the otherwise stark white wall.

"Did he hurt you, your uncle?"

"Yes," I said. Though it wasn't really true. He hadn't physically hurt me in a while.

"How long has he been hurting you?"

I looked up at the officer through cold, dead eyes. "Ever since I've lived with him," I said.

"How long has he been doing… sexual things to you?"

"Months. Almost a year."

My mother gasped. Up until that point I hadn't even noticed her standing in the corner of the claustrophobic room. The officer nodded and glanced at her. "Thank you," he said to me.

After he left, I threw up. My mother held my hair, patted my back, held the emesis basin under my mouth. Her touch made my skin crawl, made me want to throw up even more.

"Where's Kenny?" I asked once I'd emptied my stomach. I lay back on the examining table and stared at the bright light above my head.

"The police are talking to him at the house. You did real good, Chrissy. I'm sure they won't arrest Kenny now."

"I told the truth." *Unlike you've ever done,* I thought.

"I know. I'm sorry, Chrissy. I never thought..."

I blocked her meaningless words out, closed my eyes, and replayed the only words I wanted to hear in my head in my uncle's voice, "I love you, Chrissy. I love you, Chrissy."

Then I drifted off to sleep.

***

I woke up in another hospital room, unsure of how much time had passed. My mother was there asleep in a chair. I wanted to get up and leave, to go home and see if maybe it'd all been a dream. Maybe he wasn't dead. Maybe he was waiting for me with a new book or a new dress. Waiting to tell me how much he loved me.

I tried to get up, but I felt so weak. I leaned over the side of the bed and heaved and gagged, but nothing came up. I was empty. My mother woke up and was by my side in seconds. I swatted her away from me as I began to wail, thoughts crammed every part of my brain: where was Kenny now? Was he still talking to the police? I wanted my Uncle Teddy. I wanted to go back home.

I screamed and cried until a nurse came in and gave me a shot. Then I drifted off to sleep again.

***

I lost track of time in that hospital. I never really figured out how long I stayed there, because I spent most of those days unconscious. And that was fine with me. The less I was awake, the less I hurt. The day I was discharged, Mama told me that Kenny was at a juvenile center. She said they sent Kenny to juvie because although he had killed our uncle to protect me, he still obviously had a violent nature and had expressed a hatred for white people in general. They had locked him up for the safety of the public. I thought a more truthful reason was that it was 1973, racism was still very much alive, and my half-black brother had killed a white man. "He'll only be there for a few months," she said. I thought to myself that the only person who deserved to be locked away was her, not Kenny.

She made a fuss over helping me get dressed in the new clothes she bought me. She brushed my hair and smiled at me lovingly. Her good mother act made me so angry. "You're not pregnant, so that's good. Then again, I always thought Teddy was sterile, anyway, since the mumps came down on him when we were kids. That's probably why he didn't believe Tabitha's kids were his," she informed me. "I guess you just have a nervous stomach. I had a nervous stomach when I was a girl."

I closed my eyes and sighed. I wished she'd shut up.

"Henry will be so happy to see you. He won't believe how you've grown."

I frowned. "I'm not going anywhere with you," I said as I pulled my shoes on.

"What?"

I sucked in a deep breath and this time I screamed the words. "I said, I'm not going anywhere with you!"

"Chrissy—"

A nurse burst into the room. "Is everything okay in here?"

Mama nodded. "We're fine. Just a little misunderstanding."

The nurse glanced at me and left.

"I'm not going anywhere with you," I repeated more calmly this time. "Take me home."

"Surely you don't want to go back there."

I stared at her.

"Fine, we need to go get your stuff anyway."

When we got to the house, I went straight to my uncle's room, removed the yellow tape from the doorway, stepped over the blood stain, and crawled into his bed. I pulled the covers over my head and closed my eyes. Minutes later, I heard my mother's voice buzzing in my ear like an annoying fly. "Chrissy, I understand how you feel. He could be so mean and he probably really hurt you the first time, but... but after that, when he touched you, he would be so gentle, so nice. It's confusing, I know, but what he did was wrong. It was wrong when he did it to me. But it was even more wrong when he did it to you."

I didn't say a word or move a muscle.

"I don't know what was wrong with me, leaving you with him. I should've known he'd hurt you eventually. I'm so sorry." Her voice quaked with every word.

I snatched the covers off my head. "*Eventually?* He was *always* mean to us, was always beating us. You *knew* he was mean. You knew he hated us and you still left us with him."

"I didn't have a choice. Henry—"

I sat up straight. "Stop lying! You were just scared I'd tell about your affair! I wouldn't have told. I can keep a secret. But I guess you know that now, don't you?"

"Chrissy—"

"He wasn't mean anymore. Things were so much better, but now he's gone. Why did you have to come here and mess everything up?" I fell back on the bed as the tears came.

"Things will be good in Milwaukee."

"I'm not going."

"You can't stay here."

"Yes, I can. Send me the money you used to send to him and I can stay."

"You're just thirteen. I can't leave you alone."

"You left me alone a long time ago."

Silence.

"Chrissy—"

"I'm not leaving with you! Can't you see that I hate you?! I'M NOT GOING ANYWHERE WITH YOU!"

She stood from the bed. "Okay, okay, we'll… we'll figure something out."

22

"Power"

She took me and a bunch of new clothes and hair bows to Aunt Joyce's house, and Aunt Joyce and Yusef welcomed me with open arms. They were kind to me, treated me like the child they would've had if that bearded man hadn't messed up Aunt Joyce's body when he attacked her. I would've liked being there if I could've. The three of us would go for rides through the countryside and every Sunday after church, we'd have hamburgers and shakes for dinner. Every other day, Aunt Joyce would throw down in the kitchen—pig's feet, greens, chicken and dumplings. Her fried fish was even better than Grandma Orene's! I gained weight while I was there, really filled out. I took a bath every day and Aunt Joyce taught me how to put on makeup and take care of my hair. But despite all of that, I could never shake the sadness and I missed my brother terribly. He was in juvie for protecting me and I felt bad about that. I also missed Uncle Teddy. I missed his funeral, but I heard that not many people showed up—not even Aunt Tabitha or my cousins. They said only a few coworkers were there, them and the grandparents I'd never laid eyes on.

I lost count of how many times Aunt Joyce tried to get me to talk about what happened to me. She was always so gentle, told me she understood what I was going through, but that wasn't true. The man who hurt her hadn't spent years treating her like she was less than human. He hadn't changed the way he treated her just because she grew some breasts and hips. He hadn't taken her virginity, and he wasn't her uncle. So despite her gentleness and kindness, I wouldn't talk about it. I was still confused and very hurt about the whole thing and the last thing I wanted to do was relive it.

I stayed with my aunt and her husband for more than a year before things got messed up.

It was raining that day and Aunt Joyce had gone to the grocery store. It was a Saturday, and I had been in my room reading. When I got up to pee, I saw Uncle Yusef lying in their bed, taking a nap. Something took over me when I saw him in that bed all long and swarthy and handsome. After I used the bathroom, I went into that room and stood by the bed and watched him sleep for a few minutes. I did that sometimes. Sometimes I'd stand in the doorway and watch him and Aunt Joyce sleep at night. I'd stare at his big arm that he'd drape over her waist and his face buried in her hair and wonder how it felt to be held like that. When I slept in the bed with Uncle Teddy, he never held me like that. From time to time, I'd lay awake in bed and listen to them make love and I'd smile and wish I was my aunt. On this particular day, something came over me and I found myself stripping out of my clothes and climbing into bed beside him. It was almost as if I had stepped outside of my body and was watching myself as I snuggled close and rested my hand on his chest. I breathed in his scent. He was still half-asleep when he said, "You back, baby?" With his eyes closed, he thought I was Aunt Joyce. I didn't care.

I kissed his lips and rubbed my hands up and down his body. He touched me, caressed my skin. I felt giddy as I straddled him and kissed him again.

He moaned. *"Baby,"* he said as his eyes flickered open. Then he knocked me off of him and jumped up from the bed. "Chrissy?! What are you doing?!"

I smiled. "What it look like?"

"Put your clothes on and get out of here!"

Dejected and a little confused, I grabbed my clothes and raced from the room. I ran back into my room and sat on the side of the bed— naked. My eyes filled with tears. I didn't even know why I did it. But I knew I liked it. Maybe I was the devil. Maybe I was just evil.

I was lying in my bed with the covers over my head, crying and gasping for air, when I heard Aunt Joyce return from the store. I heard Yusef's footsteps as he met her in the kitchen. I heard their muffled voices as they spoke, and I knew they were talking about me. I heard the door to my room open. I felt someone sit on the side of my bed, smelled the sweet scent of perfume. "You wanna tell me what happened? Did you do what Yusef said? Is he telling the truth?"

Aunt Joyce was a good woman. She wasn't just taking his word as the truth. She wanted to hear my side. I could've easily lied, said he tried to rape me. But she loved him and he was a good man, so through my tears I said, "Yes, it's true. I'm sorry."

"Why, Chrissy?"

"I... I don't know. I guess I like him."

She sighed. "I really wanted to help you. I love you, honey, but you can't stay here anymore."

"I know."

***

By then, my mother and Mr. Henry had separated. She never said why they split up, but I was pretty sure he'd caught her cheating on him, because I was almost positive she never stopped cheating on him. She picked me up from Aunt Joyce's house in England and took me to a little house she was renting in Little Rock. Kenny was out of juvie and had been living there for a few months. He was thirteen and I was fifteen and we still had to share a room. I wished I hadn't tried to mess around with Uncle Yusef. This was the last place on earth I wanted to be, but what choice did I have? Where else could I go?

Mama was nice, no crazy mood swings or anything, but I guess that was because she felt guilty. And Kenny was different, too. It wasn't just that he was quiet. It was that he was *strange*. When he did talk, he talked to himself for the most part. He would scream in his sleep, too. When I tried to get him to tell me what was wrong, all he'd say was that things happened to him in juvie. Things he didn't want to talk about.

Mama had a live-in boyfriend who was unsurprisingly black and kind of cute, and from the way he looked at me, he thought I was cute, too. When he wasn't at work, he'd sit up late at night watching TV. Sometimes I'd sneak into the living room and watch TV with him. I liked him a lot and it didn't take long for me to decide that I wanted him. He was easy to get, too. All I had to do was take my shirt off and the next thing I knew, we were going at it. We did it five times before Mama caught us and put him out. She never said anything to me about it, never even mentioned his name again. Kenny was in his own world so I don't think he even realized the man was gone.

Things were like that with Mama. I did what I wanted—called her by her first name, barely went to school, and slept with every boyfriend she brought to the house. I never had a hard time convincing them to do it because either all Mama was attracted to were low-lifes, or because I was just that pretty. Those men were always giving me gifts, too. That's when I figured out I must've been good at sex and by then I actually liked it.

Eventually, Mama stopped bringing men home. She even started going to church. I refused to go with her and had stopped praying and believing around the time Uncle Teddy made me a woman, but Mama prayed all the time. I guess she thought she could pray the demon out of me. As far as I was concerned, the only person she needed to be praying for was herself.

23

"Shining Star"

1975

I never really liked boys my own age. As a matter of fact, I once overheard one of my mother's church friends saying Uncle Teddy had ruined me, that I would probably always only want to be with older men and that that was why I was so loose sexually—because of Uncle Teddy. What upset me most was the way they were talking about my uncle, because in my heart, I still believed he was the only person who'd truly loved me. I cussed Mama out for spreading my business after that woman left. Anyway, my feelings about boys my age changed one of the rare days I actually decided to go to school when a tall boy walked up behind me in the hallway and said, "Say, can I get your number?"

I turned around, poised and ready to say something smart to him, but I couldn't. He was the handsomest boy or man I'd ever seen with caramel-colored skin and deep dark eyes. I brushed a piece of hair behind my ear and gave him a smile. "Why?"

"Cause I wanna know what it feels like to talk to the prettiest and finest girl in this school over the phone, *Chrissy Dandridge*."

My smile grew wider. Plenty of guys had called me pretty, grown men, too, but there was something different about how this guy said it. "You know my name?"

"Everybody knows your name, girl."

"Well, you're cute and all, but I don't think so." I turned and continued walking down the hall, knowing that his eyes were glued to my butt.

I liked him already, but I had learned enough about men from watching my mama and from my own experiences to know that men liked women better when they were hard to catch. All of those guys I gave myself to never stuck around or even tried to call me after my mom got rid of them. Not that I cared. I just slept with them to make my mother miserable, to punish her.

Every day for two weeks, the same boy would approach me and ask for my number. Every day I would refuse. Finally, he fell to his knees in the middle of the hallway while we were changing classes. Everyone around us stopped and snickered and pointed. He didn't seem to care as he reached for my hand and said, "Please give me your number. I'ma die if you don't."

I smiled. "Get up."

He stood and smiled down at me.

"You got some paper?" I asked.

He ripped a page from a notebook and handed me a pen. "What's your name?" I asked.

"Michael Tolliver."

24

"All About Love"

The first time he called me, we talked on the phone for hours. I loved the sound of his voice, the sound of his laughter, and when we ran out of things to say, I just loved knowing he was on the other end of the phone.

"Hey, what do you like doing, like for fun?" he asked.

The first thing that popped into my head was "have sex." But I couldn't say that. I really liked him and hoped we could mean more than that to each other. So I said, "Read." It was true. I loved to read, but not as much as I loved to have sex.

"You read for fun? That's different. What do you like to read?"

"Anything, really, but I really like reading about art and history."

"I heard you were smart. Guess it's true."

"You heard that? Really?"

"Yeah. I heard you were really smart. Barely come to school and still ace your tests. Must be all that reading."

"I guess. What do you like to do?"

"Play basketball."

"You any good at it?"

"You really don't know who I am, huh?"

I frowned. "You said your name was Michael, right?"

"Yeah, I'm like the best point guard on our team."

"Oh."

"You're a trip. But that's what I like about you. You don't care about nothing, do you?"

"Ain't never had much to care about."

"That can't be true. Everybody got something to care about. Like me, I care about my parents, my grandma, basketball."

"Hmm, I do care about my little brother. And books!" I giggled. He laughed, too.

We talked for hours that night and several other nights. And before I knew what was happening, I'd fallen in love with Michael Tolliver.

***

We had been dating for a couple of months before I invited him over to the house. Mama was so happy to see he was my own age, she invited him to stay for dinner. He and Kenny hit it off, too. Spent a lot of time talking about basketball and other guy stuff that I didn't even know Kenny liked. I hadn't exactly tried to know, either. Kenny acted so weird most of the time that I just steered clear of him.

Pretty soon, Michael was at the house all the time. When his folks got him a car for his birthday, he started taking me to school and bringing me home every day. We ate lunch together, walked to classes together. I was so crazy about him and loved being with him so much that I went from sporadically attending school to having perfect attendance.

We'd been together almost a year before we said the word "love" to each other. A month later, we skipped school one day and went to his parents' house where we made love for the first time in his little twin bed. I truly didn't know what happiness felt like until I met and fell in love with Michael Tolliver. That day, as I lay in his arms in his room with the walls plastered with Dr. J and Kareem Abdul Jabbar posters, I told him about my life before I met him. I told him how my parents had both abandoned me in different ways, how my uncle had abused me and loved me all in the same breath. How my little brother had saved me and at the same time, lost himself. He listened, told me he was sorry for my past. "But I love you, Chrissy. I'll never leave you and I'll never hurt you. I promise. One day, I'm gonna be a pro basketball player and anything in the world you want will be yours. I'm gonna marry you."

I believed him. I had never believed anyone as wholeheartedly as I believed him.

Two months later, I realized I was pregnant. I was almost sure of it. My period was late and my period was never late. I was more shocked than anything. I'd had more unprotected sex than I could keep track of and at that point, I actually thought I couldn't get pregnant. I'd thought that maybe Uncle Teddy had damaged me in some way when I was younger like the man with the beard had damaged Aunt Joyce. I'd thought wrong.

When I told Michael, he had the expected myriad of emotions and reactions, shifting from surprise to trepidation and finally, to acceptance. He told me he'd meant what he said, that he'd never leave me, that we'd always be together. That promise became my lifeline.

Our parents were upset; my mother even tried to raise her voice a little when she found out. When I said, "At least it's not my uncle's baby," she quickly shut her mouth. The next thing I knew, she was buying baby stuff. Kenny didn't have much to say until one night when we were in our bunk beds supposed to be asleep. I was about six months along then. "You picked out a name?" he asked through the darkness.

"Not yet," I answered.

"You want a girl or a boy?"

"I hope it's a boy and that it looks like Michael."

"Why not a girl who looks like you?"

"A girl who looks like me will have a bad life, Kenny."

"Why you say that?"

"Look at *my* life."

"It doesn't have to be the same for your baby. You wouldn't leave her with someone like Uncle Teddy, would you?"

"No! Never!"

"See, that's what I'm saying. You just gotta make sure she has a good life."

"Yeah, I guess you're right."

"You love Michael?"

"Yeah, I do."

"Good. He's a good guy. I hope you two stay together forever."

"Me, too. Kenny?"

"Yeah?"

"Will you ever tell me what happened in juvie?"

I heard him sigh and turn over on the top bunk. "A lot of bad stuff. Stuff I can't forget."

"Maybe if you talk about it, you can forget it."

There was silence for a long while. I'd almost drifted off to sleep when he said, "I was skinny, smaller than most of the other boys. They would pick on me, push me, shove me. They knew I was in there for killing someone and one of the guards told me they were trying to see how tough I was. They wanted to make me fight but at first I wouldn't.

"They kept trying. They'd jump on me in the shower. Punch me in the stomach when I was asleep, throw food at me in the chow hall. There were some evil kids in that place. At one point, I don't think there was a part of my body that wasn't bruised up and sore. One day, I had had enough. I decided I was gonna whoop the next guy that laid a finger on me. I was sitting at the lunch table eating and I felt a hand on my shoulder and I just lost it. I picked up my tray and hit the kid in the face. He fell to the floor and I kicked him and punched him until they pulled me off of him. When I finally calmed down, I realized he was this new kid that had just got there the day before. He'd never laid a hand on me. I almost killed him, Chrissy. He lived, but I messed him up bad, broke his nose.

"When I go to sleep at night, I can hear him crying and yelling for me to stop. Sometimes I can feel those other guys hitting me and stuff, too. Anyway, they moved me after that. I never even got a chance to tell that kid I was sorry. But one good thing was no one bothered me at the new place."

I lay there for several minutes before saying, "I'm so sorry, Kenny. I'm sorry you went through all of that for helping me. You saved me, Kenny. I don't think I've ever thanked you for that before, but thank you."

"I'd do it again. He was evil and he deserved to die. That night when I tried to tell Mama what was going on and you lied about it, I knew I was going to have to do something because he had your head all messed up. I did what I had to do for you, for *us*. Far as I'm concerned, it was worth it, Chrissy. No matter how many nights I got my butt kicked, it was worth it."

Tears filled my eyes. "I love you, Kenny Ray, Jr."

"I love you, too, Chrissy."

25

"Keep Your Head to the Sky"

We were sitting in Michael's car in front of my house that day. He had just brought me home after school and I was waiting for him to climb out of the car and open my door for me like he usually did. Several minutes passed as he sat and stared straight ahead. He'd acted strange at school that day, too, but exams were coming up and I figured he'd been studying hard to keep his grades up and was just tired.

"Michael?" I said.

No answer.

I began to wonder if he was so tired that he'd fallen asleep with his eyes open. My Uncle Larry used to do that sometimes. Finally, I reached for the door handle. I was huge and my feet were swollen and I really wanted to crawl into bed.

"Wait, I gotta tell you something," he mumbled.

"What?" I asked.

He shifted his eyes to me and there was so much pain in them, I knew I didn't want to hear what he had to say. "We're moving."

I frowned slightly. "Y'all got a new house?"

"Yeah... in California."

My stomach dropped. I hadn't thrown up since I first got pregnant, but at that moment, my lunch was slowly marching its way up my esophagus. "What?"

"We're moving. We're moving next month."

I uttered the only words that were floating in my head. "You're moving before the baby is born? But you promised..."

"Chrissy, I'm sorry, baby. You know if it was up to me, I wouldn't go. I just don't have a choice. My dad's company is moving us." His voice was somewhere between a beg and a whine.

I shook my head and wrapped my arms around my stomach. "They hate me. Your parents hate me. They always have. They're doing this on purpose."

"No, they don't and this has nothing to do with you. It's about his job."

"No, they want us apart and you know it."

"No—"

"You think I don't know they hate me? I'm not stupid, Michael!"

Silence.

"What am I supposed to do? I can't have this baby alone. I can't!"

"I'll… I'll come back and be with you when you have the baby."

"How? They're not gonna let you come back to Arkansas and you know it."

"Maybe they will."

I shook my head. "They won't."

"Just… just wait for me. Please wait for me, Chrissy."

"Wait for you? How can I wait? When it's time for the baby to come, it's gonna come. I can't stop it."

"I don't mean that. I mean after that. Wait for me. I'll come back for you and the baby when I can."

I frowned as I looked into his eyes. "How long am I supposed to wait? Until you graduate from high school? College? Go pro? Two years, six years? How long?!" My face was heating up, my head felt like someone or something was squeezing it.

"I love you. We can still talk on the phone and send letters. We can keep in touch. Just believe in us. I haven't even moved yet and you're already giving up."

I gagged, pushed the car door open, leaned my head over the driveway pavement and heaved up part of my lunch.

"Chrissy! You okay?"

I shook my head as I stepped out of the car and made my way to my house. "No."

***

My baby girl was born in the heat of summer. She came out red-faced, kicking and screaming, demanding the attention of everyone around her. I realized very quickly that this child would not be ignored. I named her Mona-Lisa because, while some babies come out looking like wet rats, Mona was beautiful from the second she entered the world; she was a work of art. It was as if she'd inherited the best features that Michael and I had to offer.

She was so beautiful that people would go to the nursery window to see other babies and end up doting on her—a crowd-drawing beauty, she was. I was so proud of her. I just knew in my heart that once me and the baby could be with Michael, we would the perfect family. I loved being a mother in the beginning. It felt so good to know there was someone in the world who loved me and depended on me for everything. When school started back, my mother kept her. By then she'd moved a new boyfriend in and he was paying the bills so she didn't have to work. I guess she figured I was too preoccupied to set my sights on him. She was right.

I didn't mind Mama keeping her because from the moment Mona was born, my mother fell in love with her, treated her better than she ever treated me. But then again, even as an infant, Mona kind of demanded respect from those around her. Kenny fell in love with her, too. His eyes would light up when he was around her and he loved holding her and talking to her. She seemed to light all of our lives up and everyone was crazy about her—well, everyone except Michael's parents who never tried to visit her and wouldn't allow Michael to, either, and I really missed him. They didn't even send her a card or a present, but I wasn't really surprised because like I told Michael, I knew how they felt about me, what they thought of me. They had money and were also very Afrocentric and educated, and there I was, a mixed girl with curly hair, green eyes, and light skin, a girl from the country with an accent to match. A girl of more-than-humble beginnings who still had to share a bedroom with her brother, a girl who was poor by any standards. A girl known for being pretty and skipping school who'd gotten herself knocked up by their son, potentially ruining his future. I knew that was how they felt about me, that they saw me as beneath Michael, beneath *them*. But what they didn't understand was that I was just as invested in his further as they were, as he was. After all, I was going to be his wife. He'd promised me that.

26

"After the Love Has Gone"

I sent Michael letters and pictures of me and Mona every day so he wouldn't forget about us. He called me every night sounding sad. He obviously missed us and that made me feel better about the situation. I tried to ignore the hole in my heart that was left behind by his absence. I tried to go about my day and take care of our daughter and hold on to the hope of us being together again, but a few months after he left, around which time his phone calls decreased from daily to weekly, I all but gave up. A little later, he stopped calling altogether and after that, I stopped sending the letters and pictures. I never thought about his side of things. All I could see and feel was the familiar pain and loneliness of having been left behind by someone I loved and depended on. I became angry. I began to see Mona as a burden and a reminder that if I opened my heart, it would only be broken. Every wound that had scarred over because of Michael's love burst open and began to bleed and ooze and fester. Soon, I hated him. I hated myself. I hated my life.

What do you do when you're miserable? You make everyone around you miserable. Misery not only loves company, misery seeks it out. Misery creates more misery. Misery feeds on itself.

I became a bitter, hellish person. I was unbearable to be around and I knew it. And I didn't care. I screamed at everyone—my mom, Kenny. I thought Mama deserved any rage I could give her but I hated how I treated Kenny. It was like I lost control of myself. I couldn't stop being angry.

When Michael finally called again, I wouldn't hear anything he tried to say. I yelled and screamed into the phone, said horrible things to him, things no man would want to hear. Things I hoped made him feel like less than a man. And then I told him to never call me again, *ever*. He called back so many times I lost count. I hung up in his face every time. At the time, I hated him more than I hated my Uncle Teddy, and that's a lot of hate.

***

I eventually stopped going to school and spent most of my days in bed. I moved out that next January and got my own Section 8 apartment and survived on welfare and food stamps. My mother still kept Mona from time to time and she'd buy her diapers and little dresses. She'd gotten married to her boyfriend and since I'd left, she seemed happier so I made sure to give her hell every time she came over or every time I went over to her house. I still despised her and believed she had no right to be happy, especially since I was so unhappy. I remember once when Kenny tried to reason with me, but I wasn't trying to hear it.

"You should be nicer to Mama. She's different. She takes medicine and stuff so she doesn't get mad much anymore. Besides, you two might need each other one day," he said; he was holding Mona in his lap. She was playing with a little doll Mama had bought her.

I laughed. "You must be crazy. I ain't never needed her before. Why would I need her in the future? And she ain't no different. It's all an act."

He shook his head. "You're wrong."

"Have you forgotten what she did to us?

"No, but I forgave her. She's better now. She's been better for a long time now. You just too mad to see it. You mad at everybody because Mike left. I think you like being mad."

I rolled my eyes. "You *should* be mad."

"I got tired of being mad. Got tired of being sad. Got tired of being crazy and messed up and remembering that stuff."

"Well, I *can't* forget it. If what happened to me had happened to you, you wouldn't forget either. I can still smell him sometimes. I wake up with the scent of his breath in my nose." I shuddered and wrapped my arms around my body.

"Maybe I lucked out a little because he never touched me like that, but I have my own stuff to deal with, Chrissy."

I suddenly felt stupid for the things I'd said. Kenny had been through so much and he went through most of it for me and I'd been so mean to him. My rage and anger had been so wide and sweeping that it had covered my love for the one person who knew and loved me the most. "I know. I'm sorry. I'm just pissed about everything, I guess. I love you, you know?"

"Love you, too. Give her a chance, okay?"

I nodded. "I'll try."

Two weeks later, at the age of fourteen, Kenny left for school and didn't return home.

27

"Spread Your Love"

It was 1977. There was no such thing as an Amber Alert or a Morgan Nick alert. There were no cute little ID cards with a kid's name and fingerprints on them. There were no 24-hour news outlets spinning tales of missing children and soliciting help to find them. Kenny was a fourteen-year-old black boy—because in America, biracial is the same as black if one of the races is black—and no one cared about him going missing. My mother called the police, but they didn't canvas the neighborhood. They didn't do a big search with helicopters or dogs or the FBI. There were no clues, no witnesses. It was as if he vanished into thin air.

To make matters worse, because of his age and history, the authorities labeled him a runaway and told my mother he would probably be back sooner rather than later. They were wrong and I never saw or heard from my brother again. His disappearance was a mystery that haunted me for the rest of my life.

Kenny's absence broke me in a way that I cannot explain. It was like the last little string that held my soul together snapped. Like everything that I was, everything that I knew to be right and good, just disappeared, leaving a hollow, empty place inside of me that was never filled again. The only way I could cope was to pretend that Kenny never existed, to totally erase him from my mind, and that was what I did. I acted like there had never been a Kenny. I guess my mother adopted the same method of coping because after she drove around Little Rock plastering every telephone pole she could find with flyers, after she pleaded with newspapers and TV stations to interview her, after she fell to her knees in hours of prayer, after she eventually gave up finding him, she stopped mentioning him. She boxed up his stuff and put it in storage. Then she went on with her life with her husband. I envied her. At least she still had someone. I had no one but a baby who depended on me for everything and I had nothing left to give her.

As time pressed on, in a further attempt to erase both him and the pain of his absence, I started leaving Mona with my mom on Friday and Saturday nights and going to clubs. At first, I was too young to get in, but I quickly learned that a little flirting could get you into anywhere you wanted to be and following through on the flirting could get you even more. I slept with bouncers, bartenders, random guys I met on the dancefloor, anyone and everyone. My only rule was: *no white men*. White men reminded me of Uncle Teddy. But a black man? I would sleep with a black man at the drop of a hat, especially if he looked like Yusef.

I didn't love any of those men. I didn't want to love any of them, because Michael Tolliver had shown me that love was a stupid waste of time, that what Aunt Joyce had told me about men so long ago was true—they weren't good for anything except what they could give you. The guys didn't know I didn't love them. I mean, I never said I did, but I never said I didn't, either. Shoot, I was fine with an anonymous one night stand. They were the ones who'd beg for my number, try to turn quick sex into a relationship. They would buy me things—clothes, shoes, jewelry. They'd buy stuff for Mona, say they wanted to be her father. But that never lasted long, because as soon as they turned their backs, I'd have another man in my bed. I wasn't loyal to any of them. I wasn't loyal to anyone but myself.

28

"You"

I used to wonder why men wanted to be with me so badly. Besides my looks and my sex, I didn't think I had anything to offer. I had no education, no ambition. Then I decided that maybe all it took for a man to fall in love was good looks and good sex. So many of them said they loved me, a couple even asked to marry me. I would laugh in their faces, inform them that plenty of men loved me. They would leave angry and hurt, not realizing I'd already replaced them.

As time passed, I stopped going to clubs. I really didn't need to anymore. I met men in stores, at the movies, anywhere. Married men, single men, it didn't matter. As long as they gave me what I wanted and needed and numbed my pain if only for a few minutes, they served their purpose. Honestly, with a man between my legs, I could forget about most anything. But by the time I was nineteen, things had gotten a little out of hand. Men I'd never met would knock at my door all times of the night, upsetting whatever man I had decided to spend time with. My main men were paying my bills, so these strangers showing up out of the blue, knocking or calling my phone, were bad for business. I had no idea who was giving my information out, but it was not cool, not cool at all.

Things eventually got so bad, I had to relocate to my mother's house in Jacksonville, Arkansas, where she and her husband had moved. Mona and I shared a full-sized bed in their guest bedroom. I was glad they had moved as I wasn't sure I would've been able to sleep in the room I'd once shared with my brother. I stayed there for several months, and I actually kind of liked being there. I still hated my mother, but we pretty much avoided each other so things were kind of peaceful. Her husband, my stepfather, was a nice guy, always had been. He was good with Mona, too, even though he wasn't nearly old enough to be a grandfather. He was a lot younger than my mom, but he seemed to love her, and she seemed to love him, too.

***

I was fast asleep when a sound suddenly awakened me. I wasn't sure what it was, but it was extremely loud and unsettling. As I tried to focus my eyes, I shifted my gaze to the small window in the bedroom and noticed that the sun had risen. I had no idea what time it was, but I figured I'd better get up and feed my baby girl. I reached across the bed and realized she was not there beside me and almost instantly panicked. Mona was smart, a little too smart for a four-year-old, and more than once when I had my own place, she'd wound up outside my apartment while I was asleep. I never even knew when she figured out how to unlock the door. The guy who was in my bed one of those times said I slept too late to have a kid. I cussed him out and made him leave. He was the reason I was sleeping that late anyway! It wasn't my fault.

I hopped out of bed and raced through the house calling her name and hoping she hadn't slipped outside. Then I heard the noise again—a clanging sound coming from the kitchen. I rushed into the kitchen to find both Mona and my mother's husband banging on pots and pans with spoons. I stood there confused for a moment and just watched them. Mona was giggling, her curly hair a mess all over her head. My stepfather was smiling, too, gazing down at her.

"What's going on in here?" I asked. "Sounded like the house was falling apart. Scared me to death!"

Neither of them could hear me over the racket they were making. So I yelled, "Hey!" at the top of my lungs. Both of them stopped and looked up at me with equally sheepish expressions on their faces. "What's going on?" I repeated.

My stepfather shrugged. "She woke up hungry and I fixed her something. Then I asked her if she knew how to play drums; she said no, so I decided to teach her."

I placed my hands on my hips. "Those ain't drums."

"I know," he said. "They're *pretend* drums. Didn't you ever play pretend drums?"

I rolled my eyes. "No."

"You missed out. I'll have to get on to Patty about that," he replied with a grin.

"Humph, if you gon' get on to her about my childhood, you better reserve a month or two."

His expression changed. "Look, I was just trying to show your little princess some fun. Hope you don't mind."

I cocked my head to the side. "It's okay. Any more breakfast?"

He nodded as he got to his feet. "Yeah, there's plenty. Help yourself."

I grabbed a plate from the cabinet and heaped the delicious-looking breakfast onto it. "Thank you. Shouldn't you be at work?"

As he took a seat at the table, he said, "On vacation this week."

"Then why ain't y'all vacationing?" I asked as I waved my fork around.

"Your mom got called in to work."

"Oh, yeah, I forgot about that new job of hers. She get bored being a housewife or something?"

He shook his head. "No, she just likes working at the women's shelter and helping people."

I scoffed as I took a bite of toast.

"You need to cut her some slack. I know you two had issues in the past, but—"

I held up my hand. "Look, you seem like a nice guy and everything, but you don't know nothing about me and my mama and what went on between us. I like you and I respect you. Don't say nothing to change that."

He fell silent as Mona continued to beat her drums, but a little quieter this time.

***

A couple of mornings later, they were at it again. This time, I sleepily stumbled into the kitchen to find Mona sitting on the floor, her face marred with grape jelly as she banged on a stock pot. My stepfather was sitting at the table grinning down at her. I slumped into a chair and covered my eyes with my hand.

"Did we wake you?" he asked.

I looked up and smirked at him. "What you think?"

He stared at me thoughtfully. "You hung over?"

I rolled my eyes. "Why you ask that? Why the hell I gotta be a drunk?"

He leaned back in his chair. "I didn't say you were a drunk. I asked if you were hung over. I saw the empty cans of beer in the trash. Neither me nor Patty drink."

"Patty," I scoffed. "Whatever. I'm grown, so why you hassling me about it—what am I supposed to call you anyway, 'cause I damn sure ain't calling you Daddy. My daddy is dead."

He frowned. "But Patty said he—"

"Patty is a damn liar!" I screamed.

Mona stopped banging on the pot and stared at me. I scooted the chair across the floor and stomped back to my room where I flopped across the bed and closed my eyes. I had only been lying there for a few minutes when I heard his voice. "Look, you're right. You're grown. You wanna drink and party and sleep with all those guys, it's your business."

I sat up straight and glared at him. "You don't know nothing about me. I ain't sleeping with nobody."

"Well, you've got a reputation, Chrissy, and you're breaking your mother's heart."

I stood and walked toward him. He was taller than me, so I looked up at him and said, "I hope she has a damn heart attack, then."

He grabbed my arm. "What is wrong with you? You don't mean that."

I glared at his hand on my arm. "What is wrong with *you*, putting your hands on me?"

He dropped his hand. "For as long as I've known you, I've wondered how so much hatred could live inside of such a beautiful person. You're like a gorgeous ocean full of dead fish, rotten and mean as hell for no reason."

I swept my open palm across his cheek. "And you can go to hell."

He clutched my wrist and kissed me. I kissed him back, wrapping my arms around his neck and pressing my body against his.

"Skooter," he said once our lips parted.

"What?" I asked, confused.

"Skooter, you can call me Skooter. That's what everybody else calls me."

Then I watched him walk out my bedroom door.

29

"The Speed of Love"

I didn't even know I was attracted to Skooter until that moment. I suppose I had never paid him much attention up until then. He had come into my mother's life when I was preoccupied with Michael and being in love and becoming a mother. After that I'd been too busy forgetting my brother.

But Skooter had always been there in the way an accent table or some other odd piece of furniture just sits in a room not really serving a purpose. When I came around, I was always too busy hating my mother or using her as a babysitter to pay attention to him. He was tall with ocher skin and round brown eyes. When he smiled, which seemed like all the time, he lit up the whole house. He was nice, too nice for my mother. And he was so kind to Mona, seemed to really be interested in getting to know her. He was the first of my mother's men that I didn't pursue. I'd honestly had so much sex up to that point, I was kind of burnt out with it. I was tired of men climbing on top of me without regard for my feelings. I missed being in love. But after his kiss, I knew I had to have him.

It was a long time before he touched me again, weeks. He said he was ashamed of himself. I told him not to be. I liked him a lot, maybe too much since he was married to my mother. But of course I didn't care about that.

The first time we had sex was late one night when it was just him and me and Mona in the house. My mother was out of town taking care of her sick mother. Her father was already dead by then. I was fast asleep when I felt someone shake me. When I opened my eyes, Skooter was standing over me. He didn't have to say a word because I knew what he wanted and all I wanted was to be close to him, to touch him because I had let myself fall in love with him. So I slid out of bed, leaving Mona behind. At first I thought he was taking me to his and my mom's bedroom and I was going to protest because that would've reminded me too much of doing it with Uncle Teddy. But instead, he led me out into the back yard, to a lounge chair where he sat down and beckoned for me to sit on his lap. He kissed me for a long time and when he came up for air, he said, "You think Mona is okay?"

I nodded and breathlessly said, "Yeah, she sleeps like a log."

He threaded his fingers through my hair. "Chrissy, I really do love your mother."

"I know, but you love me, too, right?"

"Yeah, I think I do."

He kissed and caressed and undressed me, and I moaned his name over and over again. "Say my real name," he requested. "Say Donald, not Skooter."

As we began to make love, I said, "Donald..."

***

I don't know why I stopped taking my birth control. Maybe I was just tired of popping pills. Or maybe it was because I'd moved back in with my mom and had no intentions of having sex with anyone. Regardless of the reason why, I had stopped taking them and two months after I became my stepfather's mistress, I realized I was pregnant. I was never scared of much as an adult, but I was scared to tell him, scared I would lose his love because of it. But when I told him, he was ecstatic, said he'd always wanted kids but had understood that wasn't an option when he married my mother. She had told him it was out of the question. No way was she having any more kids. I agreed with her. The last thing she needed to do was screw up any more kids' lives. He said that was why he enjoyed being around Mona so much; he'd thought that being a step-grandfather was as close as he would get to being a father.

As I sat on the side of my bed watching him, he paced the floor and excitedly made plans for our future, plans that included him leaving my mother for me. My heart leapt. Did he really love me that much? As he talked, I jumped up from the bed, flung my arms around him, and kissed him all over the place. Mona, who had been sitting on the floor playing with some blocks, ran over to us and giggled as she grabbed his leg. "I love you so much!" I shrieked.

Donald grinned. "I love you, too. We're going to be a family, all four of us." He bent over and kissed my belly.

30

"Here Today and Gone Tomorrow"

2012

There are some things I'll never forget.

I'll never forget the warmth and goodness and love I felt at Grandma Orene's house. I'll never forget the sight of my strong, proud aunt bruised and battered and lying in the dirt in my grandmother's front yard. I'll never forget the sting of Uncle Teddy's belt against my skin, or the tobacco stains on Aunt Tabitha's dresses, or the smell of pee that always seemed to follow my cousin, Toby, around. I'll never forget all the times Uncle Teddy raped me. I'll never forget the look on Aunt Joyce's face after I tried to rape Uncle Yusef. And I'll never forget the sight of my mother, who despite her flaws, had tried to be a better mother to me, as she stood in the doorway of her home, tears streaming down her face as she watched her husband leave her for her daughter.

31

"Build Your Nest"

1980

Donald and Mona and I moved into an apartment in Jacksonville across town from my mother's house and I was so happy to be with him! He was a neat freak so, unlike my first apartment, I tried to keep our place clean. He bought Mona some really nice furniture and for the first time, she had her own room. She'd slept on the sofa in my old apartment. We would go to the park together, eat out sometimes. He even promised to marry me once his and my mom's divorce was final.

Loving him was different from loving Michael. Michael was young, a boy really, and with being that young came limitations. He couldn't take care of me, though he wanted to. He was still under his parents' rule, so our relationship could only go so far. And he had no idea how to treat a woman because he had no experience and was not yet a man. Donald Williams was all man, *one hundred percent man*—full of maturity and patience and love, not just lust. He took care of me better than any one person ever had in my entire life. And I loved him for it.

Had my pregnancy not been a total and complete nightmare, I would have enjoyed those months in that apartment, but I couldn't. I was sick all day, every day, for the better part of the pregnancy. I was so sick that I was actually hospitalized at one point for dehydration because I couldn't keep anything down—no food, no liquids. Shoot, just smelling food and water made me sick. I vomited just about everything I ate and when I ran out of food to regurgitate, I would dry heave for hours. When Donald was at work, it eventually got to the point that Mona basically had to fend for herself. Good thing she was smart and knew how to fix her own sandwiches and cereal or else she might have starved to death since most days I only managed to crawl out of bed long enough to cook dinner. I figured that was the least I could do for my man since he worked so hard to take care of me.

When our daughter was born, I was a little disappointed because I really wanted to give Donald a son, but he was ecstatic. She was a beautiful baby. She was darker than Mona and had Donald's brown eyes instead of my green eyes. She looked almost nothing like me, and I kind of liked that. But from the moment she entered the world, I knew she was going to be a different type of child than Mona was. She never really cried but rather she whined and whimpered *all the time*, day in and day out. Nothing would seem to quiet her, either. She just whimpered like a kicked puppy or something and it was very irritating to me. I didn't understand why she would never quiet down.

Some days, when the girls took a nap, I would walk down to the corner store and buy a beer or two, just a little something to take the edge off. I finally understood why Uncle Larry would drink all the time. It helped numb me, kept me mellow. And I really needed to mellow out; taking care of that baby would've rattled a nun's nerves.

***

"Chrissy, Chrissy, wake up. You been asleep all day? You didn't hear the baby?"

I slowly opened my eyes and tried to focus on his face. "What?"

"The baby is crying and she sounds hoarse. How long you been asleep?" Donald asked, his voice laced with irritation, concern in his eyes.

I pushed myself into a sitting position, saw Mona standing in the doorway with what appeared to be mustard smudged on her cheek. "What are you doing home? What time is it?"

He frowned. "It's six o'clock. I'm off work."

I bolted to my feet. "What?! How can that be? You... you just left!"

"No, I've been gone all day. And you've been asleep all day, haven't you?"

I rushed across the room to the baby bed and wondered to myself how I'd slept through her cries with her in the same room with me. He was right, she was hoarse and red-faced and I instantly felt ashamed, like I was a worse mother than my own mother. Tears stung my eyes as I reached to pull her out of her crib. Donald blocked me with his arm. "I've got her. You obviously need some rest, so you can take your ass on back to bed."

The tears fell furiously then. I'd never heard him so angry. He was always so patient and kind but I guess his patience had run out with me. I followed him from our bedroom to the kitchen which was a mess from Mona fixing her own food. Usually, I would've cleaned all of that up by the time he made it home and be at the stove fixing dinner.

With our daughter, Cleopatra, in his arms, he stalked to the refrigerator, opened it, and closed it. He glared at me as he said,

"There're no bottles in here."

My eyes widened. "Damn, I'm sorry. I was gonna fix some this morning, but…"

He slumped into a chair and held our still-crying baby to his chest. I just stood there until he said, "You gon' fix one now?!"

I nodded and rushed to the sink full of dirty bottles.

"This was a mistake and you are my punishment for hurting Patty. She was a good wife and I hurt her and for what? I love my baby, but you… *damn*."

I didn't turn around but stood there washing bottles as tears ran down my cheeks into the sink. What was I supposed to say? That I was tired of his whining baby? That I didn't like being stuck in the house with two kids? That I wasn't even sure if I really loved him anymore? That he kind of bored me now that we were together and not sneaking behind my mother's back? No, I couldn't say any of that because he had a good job and we had a nice place, so I just washed the bottles and said, "I'm sorry."

32

"System of Survival"

I was messing things up with him. I knew I was. In my mind, I wanted to be a good mother and a good girlfriend and eventually, a good wife. In my heart I wanted to love him and Mona and Cleo. I wanted to be a good person, a better person than my mother or father or uncle had ever been. But it was as if there was a switch turned on in my brain that I couldn't shut off no matter how hard I tried. It was like an involuntary reflex for me to do the wrong thing, to say the wrong thing, to *feel* the wrong thing. I was defective, damaged goods. It seemed as though someone had accidentally stamped the word "void" on my forehead and that even after they scrubbed it off of my skin, the ink remained embedded in my flesh, marking me for failure in my own eyes. What was worse was that I was a failure in everyone else's eyes, too. Evidently, being treated like crap during your formative years has a way of screwing you up.

Donald stuck around until Cleo was two, which was much longer than I'd expected him to. I knew he wanted to leave, so I made it easy for him. One day when he was at work, I invited one of the neighbor's boyfriends over and we spent the day drinking. By the time Donald made it home that evening, we were both passed out in the bedroom. We didn't do anything, but I had stripped so I knew Donald would think we did. I heard him come in and say something to Mona and Cleo who were in the living room playing. When he came into the bedroom and saw the guy in bed with me, he exploded. He dragged the guy from the bed, punched him several times, and literally threw him out of the front door. By the time he returned to the bedroom, I had wrapped a sheet around my body and was more than a little scared. Was he going to hit me and throw me out, too?

He stood in the doorway and stared at me, his eyes blazing with a combination of anger and pain. Then he walked over to the closet, grabbed a duffel bag, and began shoving his clothes into it while I stood against the wall and watched. As he zipped the bag, I said, "You ain't gonna say nothing? You just gonna leave?"

"The hell you want me to say, Chrissy? Huh?" He moved toward me, duffel bag in hand.

"I don't know."

"You don't know nothing, do you? Nothing but how to mess things up." He stepped toward the bedroom door.

I didn't respond to that because I happened to agree with him. "You not taking Cleo?" I asked.

He turned to look at me. "No, I have to work. I can't keep her."

"You going back to my mother?"

"No. That's over. I messed up too bad to go back."

"We're over, too?"

"What do you think? You think it's okay for me to work and take care of you and two kids, one of which ain't even mine, and let you cheat on me?! It's bad enough that you don't cook or clean, and that you got your six-year-old daughter raising my baby, but this? You took it too far. You disrespected me in my own home!"

"I... I can't help how I am."

He shot across the room and was in my face in a second flat. "I don't want to hear it! I don't want to hear about what your mother did or didn't do or how your father left! I don't want to hear it. *I* didn't do that stuff to you! You are a grown ass woman and you need to let this stuff go! You need to learn how to treat a man like a man!"

"You can't yell at me like that and you can go straight to hell if that's how you feel! You don't know me like that!"

"I know you are a sad, sorry excuse for a woman! I know you're not even half the woman your mother is!"

I slapped him as hard as I could. "Don't you ever compare me to her!"

"Oh, I've been comparing the two of you for a long time! She's better, Chrissy. Better at *everything*."

"Ha! Real funny. You think I don't know I'm better at sex than her? Too many guys have already told me that I am."

He shook his head. "Always about sex with you, isn't it?"

I frowned slightly. "No, I look better than her, too."

"Yeah, you do, but at least she has a heart. I don't know what that is beating inside your chest."

I placed my hands on my hips. "I must have something going for me. After all, *Stepdaddy*, you left her for me."

He gave me a smirk and said, "You do. You were right the first time. All you got going for you is what's between your legs."

I jumped him, pulling his coarse hair, scratching his face, biting the hand he tried to block my blows with. I screamed and shrieked as my daughters stood in the doorway, confused and crying. He pushed me until I landed on the bed and then he pinned me down. "You know what? I love you. I really do, but loving you is too hard because you don't know how to love back. You don't know how to love *anyone* back. Not me. Not your girls. I bet you don't even love that guy whose ass I just kicked. You're too messed up to love anyone."

"You're just saying all of this because you think my mother is some ray of sunshine. She's not. She let a lot of bad stuff happen to me. She's why I'm the way I am."

He shook his head. "You're the way you are because you choose to be this way. You chose to be with me, you chose to cheat on me, and you could choose to let all that stuff from the past go if you wanted to." He raised up off of me and grabbed his bag. As he walked toward the door I said, "Fine, go. I knew you would eventually anyway. All you needed was a reason and I gave you one. So go ahead and leave and take your whining daughter with you. I don't want neither one of you! I done had better than you, too!"

"As many men as you've been with, you probably have."

I quickly crossed the room and spit in his face. He wiped his face with the sleeve of his shirt, bent over and kissed both girls on the forehead, then he looked at me. "I'll pay the rent until you can find a job and I'll be back to check on Cleo. I'm not gonna take her away from her mother. A girl needs her mother."

After I heard him close the front door, I mumbled, "I wish you would. I wish you'd take both of them."

***

Cold water splashed against my body, jolting me from a foggy sleep. I shuddered and jerked to the right as I opened my eyes. I looked up at the water that rained down on me and tried to figure out what was going on. What was I doing outside in the rain?

"Ah, you're awake now," she said. I shifted my eyes to her and tried to make out her face, but the haze of the cheap liquor I'd had for dinner the previous night was obstructing my view.

"Thanks for helping me get her in here. I can handle it from here," she said to someone.

I squinted my eyes and was finally able to make out both faces and bodies—my mother and Donald. Donald gave me a pitying look, gently kissed my mother on the cheek, and left the room. I shifted my gaze to my surroundings and realized I was in the shower in my apartment. "What are you doing?" I muttered. If I'd had the energy, I would've asked Donald the same thing before he slipped away. Actually, I probably would've cussed him out.

"Waking you up," she said as she adjusted the spray of water, causing it to pelt down on me with increased intensity.

"I'm up! I'm up! *Damn!*" I said as I tried to get to my feet, but my legs were like rubber.

"How much did you drink last night?"

"Enough." I raised my hands and rubbed my arms. Every inch of my body was sore and cold. "What are you doing here?"

"Mona called me, said she and Cleo were hungry and you wouldn't wake up."

My stomach lurched and that cheap liquor threatened to show its face again. I clutched my gut and closed my eyes and when I opened them again, my mother was handing me a small trash can. I snatched it from her. "Turn the water off," I ordered.

She shut it off and said, "I bought you some groceries, fed the girls, and put them down for a nap."

I shrugged. "What you want me to do? Clap my hands? Say, 'Good job, Patty?'" I rubbed my throbbing head. "I need a damn cigarette."

"When did you start smoking?" she asked.

"None of your business."

She sighed as she took a seat on the toilet and stared at me.

"What?" I asked as I clutched the trash can and willed myself not to vomit. I didn't want to waste the energy. It seemed I'd spent the better part of my life throwing up and I was still full of foul, spoiled things. I was rotten on the inside, just like Donald said.

"I'm just sitting here thinking about your father, wondering what he'd think of you now, what he'd think of how you're living your life."

I rolled my eyes. "Well, since he's dead, I guess we'll never know."

Her eyes widened in shock.

"You honestly thought I didn't know? You are such a coward. A real mother would've told her children and tried to help them deal with it. But I had to overhear you telling Henry about it."

"I didn't think it'd do you any good to know."

I chuckled bitterly. "Yeah, because you were always so concerned about what was good for me, right? What are you here for, anyway? To gloat because Donald left me? To rub it in my face that I messed things up with him? Y'all back together now?"

She shook her head. "No, we're not getting back together and I'm here because you are my daughter and I love you."

I threw the trash can at her. "Get out of here!"

She dodged it and yelled, "I'm just trying to help you!"

I struggled to my feet, nearly slipping on the water. "I don't need your help now! When I needed some damn help, where were you?! Huh?! Where the hell were you?!" Bitter tears swarmed every inch of my eyes. I fought them back. The last thing I wanted to do was to cry in front of her. I couldn't bear giving her the satisfaction of seeing me break down.

"*I'm sorry!* How many times do you want me to apologize? I forgive you for what you did with Donald. I forgive you for all of the men, for everything! I forgive you because you are my child and I love you, Chrissy. Why can't you forgive me? I made mistakes, but I love you so much!" She lowered her head, dissolved into tears.

I stood there in a shower-soaked t-shirt and panties and stared at her. I believed she was sorry. I believed she meant what she said. But my own pain superseded any compassion I could've possibly summoned to give her. I leaned against the back of the shower wall and finally let my own tears fall. "It hurts. It still hurts so bad. I can still feel Uncle Teddy sometimes. I can still feel him hitting me. I can hear him calling me names and the next second I can hear him saying how much he loves me. I can... I can feel him touching me. Do you have any idea how confused I was? One minute he hated me and the next he loved me and I wanted to be loved so bad, I believed him. I'm all messed up in the head because of him! How can I forgive you? *How?* You knew what he was and you *still* left me with him!"

She looked up at me with misery and regret in her eyes. "I'm... so... sorry. I know I wasn't a good mother and I made some bad mistakes when it came to you and your brother. Everything is my fault. Please forgive me."

I slumped back down to my original position on the shower floor. "I can't forgive you. I just can't. I can't forgive you, I don't love you, and I'm not your daughter. I'ma sleep with the next man you bring around me. I'ma do everything I can to hurt you the way you hurt me. You shoulda gotten locked up, not Kenny! I h... hate you. I hate you so much." I covered my face with my hands and sobbed loudly.

"You can hate me and you can hurt me, but I still love you. If you won't be my daughter, will you just let me be your mother? That's all I want to do, Chrissy. I just want to be your mother. You're all I have left. You're all I have left..."

I wiped my tears, looked up at her wet, reddened face, and for the first time, I saw my mother through eyes of empathy instead of eyes of hatred. I saw how fragile and frail she was. I saw the pain in her eyes, the damage Uncle Teddy, her own brother, had done to her. I realized that she and I were not so different, that there was a bond between us that was unmistakable. A bond of shame and brokenness that held us together like super glue. In her eyes, I also saw a reflection of my own pain, and almost against my own will, I said, "Okay," because more than anything in the world, I'd always wanted and needed a mother and she was the only one I had.

33

"They Don't See"

1992

I turned over in bed and rolled my eyes at Orlando who was lying next to me, fast asleep. I'd called him because my light bill was past due and I knew he was good for the money but I didn't count on him spending the night and I really wasn't in the mood to be around him that long. A quickie with the money left on my dresser was what I was counting on. He'd had other plans.

I lifted his arm from my waist and climbed out of bed. I didn't try not to wake him up. As a matter of fact, I made as much noise as I could, thumping things around on the dresser, slamming drawers shut. He never moved a muscle. He was sound asleep despite the fact that he had a wife and five kids at home he needed to get back to.

I stalked through the house which was empty except for me and my unwanted guest. My girls had already left for school. I plopped down on the sofa and looked around at my surroundings—dirty floors, dirty furniture, trash stacked to high heaven in the kitchen. My place was almost as big a mess as my life and I was tired. I was tired of it all. I was tired of the men, tired of them using me while I used them. And a part of me was sad that my girls had to live with me in this place with men sliding in and out of my life, my home, and my bed. They deserved for me to make them a priority in my life. They deserved better than me or their absent fathers. After all, they were the only good things I'd ever accomplished.

I leaned back on the sofa and closed my eyes. For the first time since I was a child, it occurred to me to pray, that the answers to all of my problems were with Him. So that was what I did. I prayed to be a better person, a better mother. I prayed for the strength to leave the men and the dope and the booze alone. Most of all, I pleaded with Him to forgive me for who I was and had been for so long. When I opened my eyes, I felt lighter. When Orlando emerged from my room and announced he was heading home and wasn't sure when or if he'd be back, I took it as a sign that my prayers had been answered.

After he left, I showered and dressed and walked to the gas station right down the street from my place and bought a newspaper. I spent the day perusing the want ads. I was going to find a job and after so many years, stop selling myself to pay my bills.

Before the girls were due back home from school, I opened a package of hot dogs and started cooking them. It wasn't much of a dinner, but at least they wouldn't have to fix it themselves. More importantly, they wouldn't have to come home and find me drunk or high or in bed with some random guy. On my worst days, I would just have sex right on the couch with them wide awake. I wasn't proud of that but it was who I was. I was determined to be different now. Things were going to be better for all of us.

***

They were late coming home. Both of them.

I was pretty sure Mona was off somewhere with her little boyfriend. He wasn't much to look at, but he was nice and that was good. But Cleo was only twelve, too young for a boyfriend. *Maybe she's with Mona*, I thought. Then I told myself that Mona would've told me if that was the case, and anyway, Mona had been so preoccupied with her boyfriend, she hadn't had much time for Cleo lately. I couldn't help but worry about her a little. She'd never been this late coming home from school before and all of the other kids who rode the bus with her had already made it home as far as I could tell.

I lit a cigarette, took a slow drag, closed my eyes, and rubbed my forehead. It was getting dark and I needed to figure out what to do. But I couldn't figure anything out because my mind was muddled with thoughts of my brother and him going missing when he was just a little older than my Cleo. I didn't know how to deal with it or anything else for that matter. *This couldn't be happening again.*

I finished the cigarette, mashed it into an already-full ashtray, and that was when I saw it—a neatly folded piece of notebook paper lying on the coffee table. I wondered how I'd missed it. I stared at it for a long time because something in my soul told me that I didn't want to read it, that what was on it would be bad. But although I didn't want to read it, I knew I had to. I *needed* to.

I picked it up, unfolded it, and took in my little girl's neat penmanship. I read the words over and over again as if by sheer repetition, my eyes could rearrange or change them. After I read it for the twentieth time, I stood, walked into my bedroom which held the lingering scent of Orlando's sweat, and tucked it under the mattress of my still unmade bed. Then I walked back into the living room and lit another cigarette.

She had run away.

That was what the note said. She was gone, tired of being afraid, tired of life with me. I stared across the dim room at nothing, my heart twisting in my chest as I realized how badly I had wanted to run away when I was her age, how much I'd hated my own mother. Was that how she felt about me? Of course it was. I had done nothing but scream at her and hit her nearly since the day she was born. And I was so sorry for that.

I didn't cry. My tears had dried up years earlier. I just sat there until the room became pitch black from a lack of sunlight. *Maybe I should call someone*, I thought, *but who?* I hadn't talked to my mother since she moved out of state a couple of years earlier. I hadn't talked to Donald in years and had no idea where he was. When Cleo asked me where he was, I'd told her the first place that came to mind—Milwaukee—but of course I was lying. The police? Maybe. *No, she'll be back. She has to come back. She has to,* I thought.

When the phone rang, I eagerly answered it, hoping somewhere in the back of my mind that it was her. It wasn't.

"Hey, baby! Can I come over in a few? Been missing some you."

I held the phone, not even sure who was on the other end. My mouth was so dry.

"Baby? You there?"

I rolled my eyes. "Yeah, I'm here."

"Well?"

My mind screamed *no*, told me to hang up and leave and find my little girl, but my mouth didn't get the message and instead I said, "Is this you, Cole?"

"Yeah, you know it's me. Stop playing, girl. Can I come over?"

I stared down at the spot on the table where I'd found Cleo's note. "You got any weed?"

"Hell, yeah! You know I do!"

I glanced at the empty cigarette package that lay on the table. "Yeah, come on over. Bring me some cigarettes, too."

To read more about Christina and her daughters, be sure to check out the other books in the Been So Long series.

Discussion Questions

1. Chrissy Dandridge's life was full of abuse and neglect. Do you think this affected how she treated her own children?

2. This book deals with a lot of family dysfunction that seems to have been passed down through generations. Have you ever heard of generational curses? Do you believe they exist?

3. Do you think Chrissy's life would've been better or worse if her father had never left home? If her mother had never left her with her uncle? If she and her brother had been able to stay with their grandmother?

4. Do you agree with Donald's opinion that Chrissy chose to remain a victim? Do you know anyone who has done the same thing?

5. How do you think her mother could've better helped her cope with her uncle's abuse after she found out about it?

6. The vast majority of child abusers/molesters are related to their victims. Why do you think this is?

7. Did any of your views change after reading this book?

8. Who is your favorite character in the book? What did you like most about him or her?

9. Who was your least favorite character? What did you dislike about him or her?

10. What was your favorite scene in the book? Your least favorite scene?

11. What point do you think the author was trying to get across? What do you think the overall theme of the book was?

12. How did you experience the book? Were you immediately engaged? Did it take a while to "get into it"?

13. Overall, did you enjoy reading the book? Would you recommend it to others?

14. Would you read other books by this author?

To learn how to protect your child from abuse/molestation, visit:

https://www.psychologytoday.com/blog/stop-the-cycle/201112/child-sexual-abuse-ten-ways-protect-your-kids

For information/help for incest survivors, visit:
http://www.siawso.org

If you suspect a case of child abuse or neglect, please call The Childhelp National Child Abuse Hotline: **1-800-4-A-CHILD (1-800-422-4453)**

According to the National Association of Adult Survivors of Child Abuse (http://www.naasca.org/index.html**)**, 800,000 children are reported missing every year in the U.S. (or 2,000 every day).

For more information on missing children, go to:

www.missingkids.com

For more information about Adrienne Thompson, visit:

http://adriennethompsonwrites.webs.com

Sign up for Adrienne's newsletter here:
http://eepurl.com/jnDmH

Follow Adrienne on Twitter!

https://twitter.com/A_H_Thompson

Like Adrienne on Facebook!

https://www.facebook.com/AdrienneThompsonWrites

Join Adrienne's Facebook group!!

https://www.facebook.com/groups/674088779363625/

Follow Adrienne on Pinterest!

http://www.pinterest.com/ahthompsn/

Connect with Adrienne on Goodreads!

https://www.goodreads.com/author/show/5051327.Adrienne_Thompson

Also by Adrienne Thompson

The *Bluesday* Series:

Bluesday

Lovely Blues

Blues In The Key Of B

Locked out of Heaven (Tomeka's Story – A Bluesday Continuation)

The *Been So Long* Series:

Rapture (A Been So Long Prequel)

If (Wasif's Story) A Been So Long Prequel

Been So Long

Little Sister (Cleo's Story—a companion novel to Been So Long)

Been So Long 2 (Body and Soul)

Been So Long III (Whatever It Takes)

The *Your Love Is King* Series

Your Love Is King

Better

Stand-alone novels:

Home

Ain't Nobody

See Me

When You've Been Blessed (Feels Like Heaven)

Summertime (A Novella)

Nonfiction Titles:

Just Between Us (Inspiring Stories by Women) —as a contributor

Seven Days of Change (A Flash Devotional)

All books are available at amazon.com, barnesandnoble.com, and kobobooks.com

Please enjoy this excerpt from ***Been So Long***

(Now available in Kindle, Nook, Kobo, and paperback):

In Little Rock, I slowed as I passed the office of Cardiothoracic Associates of Central Arkansas. It was the office that Dr. Wasif Masood shared with Dr. Fahad Masood, his father. Both were successful cardiothoracic surgeons, well respected in Arkansas. I slowed even more when I saw Wasif's shiny midnight blue Range Rover. I ached a little. I wished I could walk in there and surprise him. I wished I was his wife. But I wasn't his wife and wishing was a waste of time.

The blaring of car horns behind me snapped me out of my thoughts and made me realize that I'd come to a complete stop and was blocking traffic. I don't know why, but I hit my turn signal and pulled into the parking lot at Wasif's office. Maybe I just felt bold or maybe I'd lost my mind, but for whatever reason, I found myself parking in front of the office. I pulled on a pair of Fendi sunglasses, grabbed my Gucci purse, and headed into the office.

I smiled as I walked through the nearly packed waiting area and approached the receptionist's window. A blond-headed young lady returned my smile and said, "Can I help you?" Her southern accent was thick, almost comical.

I nodded. "Yes, I don't have an appointment or anything, but I was wondering if I could see Dr. Wasif Masood. He was my mother's surgeon, and I need to ask him some questions." It was a believable lie.

"Oh, well, what's your mother's name?"

"Just tell him that Mo Dandridge needs to speak with him. He'll remember me."

She shrugged and gave me a skeptical look. "Ok, but even if he agrees to see you, it may take awhile. He has a lot of appointments this morning." Wanna bet?

I nodded. "I understand."

I took the only vacant seat, which was right underneath the flat-screen TV that hung on the wall, and smiled at the rainbow of patients in the waiting area. I'd only been sitting and waiting for two minutes when she told me that he was ready to see me. I hadn't even had time to flip through the magazine I'd picked up. I thanked her as she led me to his office.

"Thanks, Paula," Wasif said to the receptionist. "Ms. Dandridge, how can I help you?"

The room smelled of the familiar scent of his cologne. I waited for him to close and lock the door, and then I smiled and whispered, "I really need your help, doctor. I missed you."

With wide eyes, he said, "Mo, what in the world are you doing here? What if my father sees you here? I'll never hear the end of it."

I pointed to the huge window behind his cluttered desk. "Then you'd better close the blinds."

He nodded. "You're right." As he turned and walked to the window, he said, "Mo, you've got to go. I'll call you later."

I looked around the office as I stepped out of my heels. Behind his huge mahogany desk sat an empty executive chair.

There were framed diplomas on the ecru wall from The University of Arkansas and the University of Arkansas for Medical Sciences. I could see a picture frame lying flat on the bookcase beside me. Probably a picture of his wife and daughters. I laid my purse in the burgundy leather chair in front of his desk, and when he turned back around, I'd stripped out of my skinny jeans and blouse and was wearing nothing but my matching pink underwear. I tilted my head to the side and gave him an innocent look. "I should go?"

He bucked his eyes as I slowly walked towards him. "Um…Mo…"

I sat on top of the desk without bothering to move any of the papers. I grabbed his hand and pulled him closer to me. He smiled. "W…what are you doing, babe?"

I kissed him softly. "I told you. I missed you, doctor," I whined.

He nodded as I loosened his tie, unbuttoned his collar, and kissed his neck. "Uh…I missed you, too, but y…you can't just show up like this, babe."

I shrugged. "Ok, doctor. I'll go then." I tried to slide off of his desk, but he blocked me.

He leaned over and kissed me as he pulled his dress shirt out of his pants. "No, Ms. Dandridge. First, you've got to finish what you've started."

"What about your patients, Dr. Masood?"

He smiled as he laid me back on his desk. "They can wait. This is an emergency."